THE GO

"And life is all swee

As Lord Warbur
his deep voice, Corena turned to look at him.

Their eyes met, and she felt as if they were speaking in the "honeyed tongues" of Olympus.

Corena had the strange feeling that Lord Warburton was thinking exactly the same thing.

There was no reason to be afraid, because they were one person, and there was nothing to divide them.

Then as the ship rolled a little more deeply, Corena put out her hand to hold on to the window ledge and came back to reality.

She was not a goddess linked to a god, but a girl caught in a wicked plot that surely doomed the promise of their newfound love . . .

A Camfield Novel of Love
by Barbara Cartland

———

"Barbara Cartland's novels are all distinguished by their intelligence, good sense, and good nature . . ."
— **ROMANTIC TIMES**

"Who could give better advice on how to keep your romance going strong than the world's most famous romance novelist, Barbara Cartland?"
— **THE STAR**

Camfield Place,
Hatfield
Hertfordshire,
England

Dearest Reader,

Camfield Novels of Love mark a very exciting
era of my books with Jove. They have already
published nearly two hundred of my titles since
they became my first publisher in America, and
now all my original paperback romances in the future will be published exclusively by them.

As you already know, Camfield Place in Hertfordshire is my home, which originally existed in
1275, but was rebuilt in 1867 by the grandfather of
Beatrix Potter.

It was here in this lovely house, with the best
view in the county, that she wrote *The Tale of
Peter Rabbit*. Mr. McGregor's garden is exactly as
she described it. The door in the wall that the fat
little rabbit could not squeeze underneath and the
goldfish pool where the white cat sat twitching its
tail are still there.

I had Camfield Place blessed when I came here
in 1950 and was so happy with my husband until
he died, and now with my children and grandchil-
dren, that I know the atmosphere is filled with
love and we have all been very lucky.

It is easy here to write of love and I know you
will enjoy the Camfield Novels of Love. Their
plots are definitely exciting and the covers very
romantic. They come to you, like all my books,
with love.

Bless you,

CAMFIELD NOVELS OF LOVE
by Barbara Cartland

THE POOR GOVERNESS
WINGED VICTORY
LUCKY IN LOVE
LOVE AND THE MARQUIS
A MIRACLE IN MUSIC
LIGHT OF THE GODS
BRIDE TO A BRIGAND
LOVE COMES WEST
A WITCH'S SPELL
SECRETS
THE STORMS OF LOVE
MOONLIGHT ON THE
   SPHINX
WHITE LILAC
REVENGE OF THE HEART
THE ISLAND OF LOVE
THERESA AND A TIGER
LOVE IS HEAVEN
MIRACLE FOR A MADONNA
A VERY UNUSUAL WIFE
THE PERIL AND THE
   PRINCE

ALONE AND AFRAID
TEMPTATION OF A
   TEACHER
ROYAL PUNISHMENT
THE DEVILISH DECEPTION
PARADISE FOUND
LOVE IS A GAMBLE
A VICTORY FOR LOVE
LOOK WITH LOVE
NEVER FORGET LOVE
HELGA IN HIDING
SAFE AT LAST
HAUNTED
CROWNED WITH LOVE
ESCAPE
THE DEVIL DEFEATED
THE SECRET OF THE
   MOSQUE
A DREAM IN SPAIN
THE LOVE TRAP
LISTEN TO LOVE
THE GOLDEN CAGE

LOVE CASTS OUT FEAR
A WORLD OF LOVE
DANCING ON A RAINBOW
LOVE JOINS THE CLANS
AN ANGEL RUNS AWAY
FORCED TO MARRY
BEWILDERED IN BERLIN
WANTED—A WEDDING
   RING
THE EARL ESCAPES
STARLIGHT OVER TUNIS
THE LOVE PUZZLE
LOVE AND KISSES
SAPPHIRES IN SIAM
A CARETAKER OF LOVE
SECRETS OF THE HEART
RIDING IN THE SKY
LOVERS IN LISBON
LOVE IS INVINCIBLE
THE GODDESS OF LOVE

Other books by Barbara Cartland

THE ADVENTURER
AGAIN THIS RAPTURE
BARBARA CARTLAND'S
   BOOK OF BEAUTY AND
   HEALTH
BLUE HEATHER
BROKEN BARRIERS
THE CAPTIVE HEART
THE COIN OF LOVE
THE COMPLACENT WIFE
COUNT THE STARS
DESIRE OF THE HEART
DESPERATE DEFIANCE
THE DREAM WITHIN
ELIZABETHAN LOVER
THE ENCHANTING EVIL
ESCAPE FROM PASSION
FOR ALL ETERNITY
A GOLDEN GONDOLA
A HAZARD OF HEARTS
A HEART IS BROKEN
THE HIDDEN HEART
THE HORIZONS OF LOVE
IN THE ARMS OF LOVE

THE IRRESISTIBLE BUCK
THE KISS OF PARIS
THE KISS OF THE DEVIL
A KISS OF SILK
THE KNAVE OF HEARTS
THE LEAPING FLAME
A LIGHT TO THE HEART
LIGHTS OF LOVE
THE LITTLE PRETENDER
LOST ENCHANTMENT
LOVE AT FORTY
LOVE FORBIDDEN
LOVE IN HIDING
LOVE IS THE ENEMY
LOVE ME FOREVER
LOVE TO THE RESCUE
LOVE UNDER FIRE
THE MAGIC OF HONEY
METTERNICH THE
   PASSIONATE DIPLOMAT
MONEY, MAGIC AND
   MARRIAGE
NO HEART IS FREE
THE ODIOUS DUKE

OPEN WINGS
A RAINBOW TO HEAVEN
THE RELUCTANT BRIDE
THE SCANDALOUS LIFE
   OF KING CAROL
THE SECRET FEAR
THE SMUGGLED
   HEART
A SONG OF LOVE
STARS IN MY HEART
STOLEN HALO
SWEET ENCHANTRESS
SWEET PUNISHMENT
THEFT OF A HEART
THE THIEF OF LOVE
THIS TIME IT'S LOVE
TOUCH A STAR
TOWARDS THE STARS
THE UNKNOWN HEART
WE DANCED ALL NIGHT
THE WINGS OF ECSTASY
THE WINGS OF LOVE
WINGS ON MY HEART
WOMAN, THE ENIGMA

A NEW CAMFIELD NOVEL OF LOVE BY

BARBARA CARTLAND

The Goddess of Love

JOVE BOOKS, NEW YORK

THE GODDESS OF LOVE

A Jove Book / published by arrangement with
the author

PRINTING HISTORY
Jove edition / July 1988

ISBN: 0-515-09644-X

Jove Books are published by The Berkley Publishing Group,
200 Madison Avenue, New York, New York 10016.
The name "JOVE" and the "J" logo
are trademarks belonging to Jove Publications, Inc.

PRINTED IN THE UNITED STATES OF AMERICA

10 9 8 7 6 5 4 3 2 1

Author's Note

Thomas, Seventh Earl of Elgin and Eleventh Earl of Kincardine, a soldier and a diplomatist (1766–1841), is famous for his acquisition of the Greek sculptures now known as the "Elgin Marbles."

Keenly interested in classical art, between 1803 and 1812 his great collection of sculptures, taken chiefly from the Parthenon at Athens, was brought to England and became the subject of violent controversy.

When he was our Envoy to the Turkish Government (1799–1803), he had bought the "Marbles" from the Turks, who at that time were still the rulers of Greece, to save them from what seemed likely destruction.

However, the Earl was denounced as a dishonest and rapacious vandal, notably by Lord Byron, while the quality of his acquisitions, later regarded as exceptional, was questioned.

In 1810 he published a memorandum defending

his actions and judgement. On the recommendation of a Parliamentary Committee, which also vindicated Elgin's conduct, the "Marbles" were bought by the nation in 1816 for £35,000, considerably below their cost to the Earl of Elgin, and deposited in the British Museum, where they remain on view.

chapter one

1899

CORENA came down the stairs humming a little tune to herself.

It was a lovely day with the spring sunshine lighting the daffodils under the trees.

The first butterflies were hovering over the lilac bushes.

She had no idea that she looked like a spring flower herself.

She was wearing a gown which matched the sprouting buds.

Her eyes, touched with gold, were the translucent green of the stream at the bottom of the garden.

She was wishing that her father were with her.

He would doubtless have quoted a Greek Ode which would illustrate his appreciation of the beauty she was seeing better than she could express in words.

However, not surprisingly, Sir Priam Melville was in Greece.

Ever since going up to Oxford, Sir Priam had had an obsession with Greece.

His outstanding and unusual knowledge of Greek antiquity had gained him a First.

Sir Priam had a Greek grandmother, so his feeling for Greece was not only in his brain but in his blood.

He had then begun to collect the statues and other relics of Greece which now embellished the beautiful Elizabethan house in which they dwelt.

It was inevitable that his daughter, when she was born, should be given a Greek name.

Also, that she would grow up to look even more beautiful than the Greek statues which both her father and mother found entrancing.

Then two years ago Lady Melville had died.

Corena had tried to look after her father, but she knew the only thing that would really help him to get over his loss was to be in Greece.

He had told her after Christmas that that was where he was going.

She thought she was lucky he had not wished to leave sooner.

She was lonely without him, but her Governess, a very intelligent woman, kept her company.

They pored over the books that filled Sir Priam's Library, and the inscriptions which had been sent to him not long before he left.

It was these inscriptions that had finally made him decide that he could stay away no longer from the land that enthralled him.

He had set off looking, Corena thought, ten years younger at the mere idea of what lay ahead.

Now, as she reached the hall, she stopped for a moment to touch an exquisite marble foot that stood on one pillar, and next to it was the head of a man.

It was a beautiful piece of sculpture and in amazingly good condition.

Her father had discovered it on his last expedition, before her mother had died, and had brought it home in triumph.

It was one of the finest examples of such sculpture he had ever seen and he could hardly believe he had been so lucky as to obtain it.

"It is fourth century B.C., my dear," he told Corena.

Corena often wondered if she would ever meet a man as good-looking or as commanding as the statue.

This morning, perhaps because it was spring, she was thinking that if she ever fell in love, it would be with a man like him—handsome, authoritative, self-possessed.

She had not found any of those characteristics in any of the young men who came to the house, or whom she had met at the few parties she attended.

Most of last year she had been in mourning and had gone nowhere.

Now she had hoped her father would escort her to some of the Balls and Receptions that were given in the County.

But he was more absorbed in the goddesses he found in Greece than in his own daughter.

'I suppose I am fortunate,' Corena often thought, 'that the women whom Papa admires so fervently have been dead for centuries, or else have retired to Olympus and no longer concern themselves with human beings.'

She laughed at the idea.

Nevertheless, Greece absorbed her thoughts also,

and her father had promised that the next time he went he would take her with him.

"Why not this time, Papa?" Corena enquired.

Her father hesitated for a moment, as if he were feeling for words.

Because she was so closely attuned to him, she asked perceptively:

"Is what you are doing dangerous?"

He looked away from her before he replied:

"It might be, and that is why, my dearest, I have to go alone."

"What are you looking for particularly?"

He had paused before he answered:

"I have heard vaguely of a statue or statues in Delphi which, incredible though it may seem, have not yet been discovered."

Corena's eyes lit up.

Anything to do with Delphi had always thrilled her.

She had read every book that had ever been written about it, and she had bombarded her father with questions.

Delphi was where the Temple of Apollo had been built beneath the Shining Cliffs, which stood a thousand feet above the pilgrims' heads, implacably stern and remote.

Her father had explained to her how when Apollo left the holy island of Delos to conquer Greece, a dolphin had guided his ship to the little town of Crisa.

Disguised as a star at high noon, the young god leaped from the ship, flames flared from him, and a flash of splendour lit the sky.

He had marched up the steep hill to the lair of the dragon which guarded the Cliffs.

When he had slain it, he announced to the gods that

4

he was claiming possession of all the territory he could see from where he was standing.

Corena dreamt of that poignant moment, and her father told her that Apollo had chosen the loveliest viewpoint in Greece.

At Delphi had been the Oracle.

People came from every part of the Mediterranean World to hear the pronouncements of a young priestess when she was possessed by the god.

Her father had a rapt admiration in his voice when he spoke to Corena of the past.

Then he would look unutterably sad as he explained that the Emperor Nero had in the first century A.D. removed seven hundred statues from Delphi and sent them to Rome.

Three years ago, French excavators had found innumerable inscriptions, ruined temples, and shrines.

But not one single statue had been left intact.

Archaeologists like her father had, however, gone on hoping, and Corena had looked at him excitedly as she said:

"Are you telling me, Papa, that you have found a statue?"

"I have *heard* of it," her father corrected her, "but it may be just a rumour. The trouble is that since Lord Elgin removed the marbles from the Parthenon, the Greeks are antagonistic towards anybody trying to carry off their treasures."

"I can understand that," Corena murmured.

"They neglected them for centuries," he said, "but now, at last, they are beginning to realise their value, even though the majority do not understand how unique and irreplaceable they are."

"And you think the Greeks might stop you from taking anything you find away?" Corena persisted.

Again her father seemed to hesitate before he replied:

"There are other men, some Greeks, some of other nationalities, who wish to exploit any findings simply for gain."

Corena understood that this was where the danger lay, and she put her arms around her father's neck, saying:

"Darling Papa, you must be very, very careful! If anything should happen to you, I would be entirely alone and miserably unhappy without you and Mama."

She saw the pain in her father's eyes as she spoke and knew how desperately he missed her mother.

"I promise I will do everything in my power to come back to you as quickly as possible," he answered, "and perhaps bringing a statue of Aphrodite, who will be as beautiful, my dearest, as you are yourself!"

Corena had loved the compliment and kissed him.

She would, in fact, have been very stupid if she had not realised she did resemble some of the more beautiful heads of Aphrodite.

Especially those carved by an Attic master in the fourth century B.C.

She had the same oval brow, the same straight, perfectly proportioned nose, the same curved chin.

Her lips, although she was not aware of it, made any man think they were made for kisses.

The few men she had met had been overwhelmed by her loveliness.

None of them, however, had appreciated that she not only had a Greek beauty, she also had the astute mind which had made the Ancient Greeks revolutionise the thinking of the world.

As she moved farther across the hall, she was thinking of her father in Delphi.

She could imagine him reciting the words of the Oracle to Julian the Apostate, who visited the shrine in A.D. 362.

He had asked what he could do to preserve the glory of Apollo.

The Oracle answered:

"Tell the King the fair-wrought house has fallen.
No shelter has Apollo, nor sacred laurel leaves;
The fountains now are silent; the voice is stilled."

"That may be true," Corena said to herself. "At the same time, however damaged Delphi may look to-day, it inspires and excites Papa, so all cannot be lost."

Because she loved her father so deeply, she felt as if she were travelling with him first overland to Italy, then by sea to Crisa.

They would look up at the Shining Cliffs and she was sure that they would see eagles flying above them.

Then the light of Apollo would leap from the ruins and her father would know that the god was no longer dead, but living.

She went into the low-ceilinged Drawing-Room where again there were many small but exquisite pieces of Greek sculpture.

A woman's hand lying open, as if in supplication.

Damaged, but still exquisite, was a statue of Eros and a plaque that depicted Aphrodite driving in a Chariot to Olympus, drawn by Zephyrus and Iris.

They were all so dear to Corena.

She dusted them daily, as her mother had done, not trusting anything so precious to servants.

She wondered what her father would find in Delphi.

Although it seemed incredible that it had not been found before, she knew he was hoping for something as sensational as the Bronze Charioteer.

He had been discovered only three years before by the French Archaeologists.

After the rubble at the foot of the Theatre had been washed away in the spring rains, a long fluted skirt and a beautifully formed foot were found.

Her father had described so often how during the following days, working with wild excitement, the French had unearthed a piece of a stone base.

Then they discovered fragments of a chariot-pole, two hind legs of horses, a horse's tail, a hoof, fragments of reins, and the arm of a child.

"At last, on May first," Sir Priam continued, "they found the upper part of a right arm some thirty feet away, closer to the Theatre."

"They were not damaged, Papa?" Corena exclaimed, knowing the answer.

"No, they were not," her father replied, "but heavily corroded by moisture from a sewer."

"It must have been very, very exciting!"

"The French were thrilled, but what surprised them more than anything else was the extraordinary state of preservation, and nothing except an arm was lost."

Corena had heard the story over and over again.

Because her father, having seen the statue later, had explained it so vividly, she could herself see the dreaming boy.

He was perhaps fourteen years old, believed to be a Prince, who had, as a Charioteer, taken part in the Pythian Games.

"Could Papa really find something like that?" she asked now.

It would be a fitting climax to his life's work and his search for the beauty and brilliance of Ancient Greece.

She went across the room to look at another piece of statuary.

Only the legs and the knees were intact, with a skillfully draped skirt above them.

So little to remain of what must have once been a perfectly shaped woman, yet even to look at it made one aware of her beauty and her symmetry.

It still inspired and stimulated, as it must have done to those who had admired the living model all those centuries ago.

Very gently, Corena touched the marble as if she caressed it.

As she did so, the door opened and the Butler announced:

"A gentleman to see you, Miss Corena!"

She turned in surprise, wondering who could be calling on her so early in the morning.

A small, sallow-skinned man came into the room.

He advanced towards her, and as he drew nearer, she could see his dark hair and even darker eyes.

Even before he spoke she guessed he was Greek.

"You are Miss Melville?" he asked with a distinct accent.

"I am."

"My name is Ion Thespidos, and I wish to talk to you."

"Yes . . . of course."

Corena indicated a chair, saying:

"Will you sit down?"

The man obeyed her and she sat in another chair opposite him, wondering why he was here.

Then suddenly, as if she realised she had been very obtuse, she stiffened as she thought his visit must concern her father.

Perhaps something had happened to him.

She did not speak, but her heart was beginning to beat agitatedly and her eyes were worried as she waited.

"You are the daughter of Professor Priam Melville?" he asked.

"That is correct," Corena managed to reply.

Then as her visitor stared at her with penetrating eyes which made her feel somewhat uncomfortable, she said quickly:

"You have come to see me . . . about . . . Papa? Has anything . . . happened to . . . him?"

"He is in no danger, Miss Melville. However, my visit does concern him."

"You know my father?"

"We met in Greece, and he is in fact—staying—with me."

There was a moment's hesitation before the word "staying."

Because Corena was exceedingly perceptive, she was aware that if this man was, as he said, concerned with her father, it was not in any circumstance of friendship.

"Will you tell me why you are here?" she asked.

"I have come to put a proposition to you, Miss Melville, and what I have to say is entirely confidential and secret."

"Yes . . . of course," Corena agreed.

Again Mr. Thespidos seemed to consider his words before he began:

"Your father is, of course, well know in Greece. He

has visited us often in the past, and has brought back with him, as I can see in this room and in the hall, some Greek treasures which in fact belong to our country!"

Corena's chin rose a little as she replied:

"You have not taken very much care of them in the past! It is only now that you are beginning to realise how important they are to the world."

"The world may appreciate them, Miss Melville, but they are ours."

As Corena had no answer to this, she thought it was best to say nothing.

She had the feeling that the Greeks, despite their apparent previous indifference, had a very good point in claiming that the glories of Ancient Greece belonged to them.

So many statues and plaques, painted pots and engravings had been dispersed to France, to England, and to other nations.

That did not, however, really justify the plunder of what were national treasures.

She remembered that German Archaeologists had uncovered the sanctuary of Olympia and had dug through an entire village to do so.

They were looking for the colossal statue of Zeus.

They never found it, but other treasures they did discover had naturally alerted other Archaeologists all over the world.

She was, therefore, silent, waiting for Mr. Thespidos to continue.

After a moment he said:

"We believe that there is somewhere in Delphi a treasure as fine as the figure of the Winged Victory, which once stood in the vestibule of the Temple at Olympia."

He paused before he went on:

"It is, in fact, a statue of Aphrodite, and so beautiful that any man who looks at it falls in love with the goddess, as he would have done when she was there."

He spoke poetically, but his voice did not sound poetical.

As Corena looked at him, she was almost sure there was something wrong, almost repulsive about him.

As she was now certain this was what had interested her father, she said nothing but waited, clutching her fingers together because she was afraid of what he would tell her.

"Your father," Mr. Thespidos went on, "has admitted to me that it is this statue of Aphrodite for which he is looking, and I believe him when he tells me it is only a rumour that it is in existence, and he knew little more."

"And you say my father is staying with you?" Corena asked.

Mr. Thespidos nodded agreement.

She had the terrifying feeling that if her father was his guest, it was on a compulsory basis, and he could not escape.

With an effort she managed to ask:

"Have you any idea when my father will return?"

"That is what I have come to talk to you about," Mr. Thespidos answered, "and it all depends on you, Miss Melville."

"On me?"

"Yes."

"Why?"

"That is what I will explain."

He bent forward as he sat in the chair so that he was a little nearer to her.

His voice dropped to a low note, so that she had to strain her ears to hear.

"I understand," Mr. Thespidos said, "that while your father had heard a rumour of this statue lying concealed in the ruins of Delphi, there is somebody else who knows a great deal more about it."

"Who is that?"

"An Englishman called Warburton—Lord Warburton."

Corena was aware of the name.

She remembered that she had heard her father speaking of Lord Warburton as a collector, as he was himself.

He had said he was a somewhat aloof man who had no acquaintance with other Archaeologists.

He did not exchange, as most of them did, his knowledge of any particular site.

As if he were following her thoughts, Mr. Thespidos said:

"Lord Warburton is a very rich man. He can well afford to pay for his discoveries, yet we have reason to think that he has stolen many treasures of antiquity from Greece, which are now in his houses in England."

"You have seen them?" Corena asked.

She had the feeling as she asked the question that it would not be easy for Mr. Thespidos to answer.

"I have not seen them," he replied, "but I have met somebody who has, and I am quite certain from his information that Lord Warburton is, in fact, a menace to Greece who should be prevented from stealing any more of our treasures."

He was speaking with what most people would have felt was a sense of patriotism and pride in his national heritage.

But Corena was convinced, even though she had no

13

grounds for substantiating it, that Mr. Thespidos was more concerned with filling his own pocket than the museums in Athens.

However, she said quietly:

"I think you must explain a little more clearly, Mr. Thespidos, what part you wish me to play in helping you, if that is why you are here."

"I will explain it very simply," Mr. Thespidos said. "If you want your father to be returned to you, Miss Melville, then Lord Warburton must take his place!"

Corena drew in her breath and stared at Mr. Thespidos before she said:

"I . . . I do not . . . understand!"

"Then I will make it clearer—I with several of my friends found your father digging late one evening in the ruins of the Temple of Athena below the Sanctuary at Delphi."

He looked at her for a moment. Then he said:

"It took us a little time to extract from him the information we were seeking—"

Corena sat upright.

"Are you . . . saying," she interrupted, "that you . . . forced or . . . tortured my father into . . . telling you what you . . . wished to know?"

"He needed a little persuasion," Mr. Thespidos replied, "but I believed him when he told me that, although he had heard a rumour about a statue of Aphrodite, he had no further knowledge of where it might be, or if indeed it actually existed."

With great difficulty Corena did not rage at him.

She knew that would not bring her father back and she would be wiser to listen first to what Mr. Thespidos had to say.

"I have, however," he went on, "ascertained from the

14

reliable source which I spoke of before, that Lord Warburton knows a great deal more about this statue than your father does."

"Then why do you not approach him?"

"He is, unfortunately, unapproachable while he is in this country, and I have heard that what he is seeking may not actually be at Delphi, but somewhere else."

"Then it does not concern my father!"

"Unfortunately, Miss Melville, Lord Warburton confides in nobody, and when he visits Greece, no one is aware that he is in the country before he has come and gone."

Corena looked puzzled, not understanding exactly what Mr. Thespidos was suggesting.

He continued:

"Greece is a country with a great number of small natural harbours where a yacht can lie hidden for perhaps a week without anybody being aware it is there."

His voice became intense as he said:

"What I therefore require from you, Miss Melville, is that you should discover where Lord Warburton will anchor, and communicate the information to me."

Corena stared at him in astonishment.

"B—but . . . that is . . . impossible!"

"Then I am afraid your father will not be returning home for a long time."

"What are you saying . . . what are you . . . trying to . . . make me do?" Corena asked.

Now, although she tried to prevent it, there was a frantic note in her voice.

She was suddenly afraid, desperately afraid for her father, and afraid, too, of the man sitting opposite her.

Now she knew without any doubt he was evil.

"Let me tell you what you have to do," Mr. Thespidos replied. "You will go to Lord Warburton and tell him your father is desperately ill in Delphi without any medical attention. The only way you can get to him is if he will convey you to Crisa in his yacht."

"And you think Lord Warburton will agree? And if he does, what then?"

Mr. Thespidos smiled, and it was not a pleasant smile.

"If you bring Lord Warburton into port at Crisa, then you can leave everything in my hands."

"Supposing he suspects that my father is a prisoner?"

"What is important is that Lord Warburton should come to Crisa, as you will be able to persuade him to do."

Corena rose to her feet.

"I have never heard anything so ridiculous in the whole of my life!" she exploded. "I do not know Lord Warburton, and it is extremely unlikely that he would concern himself in my father's illness."

"In which case, I am sure you will be very sorry not to see your father again!"

Mr. Thespidos spoke quietly, but Corena knew the "gloves were off" and now he was openly forcing her to obey him.

She wondered desperately what she could do about it.

Although he had not moved from his chair when she stood up, she felt as if he were like a huge black bird hovering over her menacingly.

He did not speak, and after a moment she said:

"What . . . you are . . . saying is . . . impossible!"

"Nothing is impossible, Miss Melville, when anyone is as beautiful as you."

Corena stiffened as she felt his insinuation was an insult.

Then she asked:

"You obviously knew what I looked like before you came . . . here."

"I could not believe that you could be as beautiful as the miniature your father carries in his pocket," he replied, "but I was mistaken! You are as lovely as Aphrodite herself, and, I am told, Lord Warburton has a *penchant* for the lady."

Corena clenched her fingers, fighting for self-control.

She wanted to scream at Mr. Thespidos and order him to leave the house.

He was not only grossly impertinent but, she thought, evil, cruel, and calculating. However, he held her father prisoner, and somehow she had to save him.

Because it was the first thing that came into her mind, she said weakly:

"I have no way of . . . getting in . . . touch with Lord Warburton, whom I do not . . . know."

She knew Mr. Thespidos would take what she said as weakness, and that she had acquiesced in his demands.

But for the moment she could not think of anything but that her father was in his clutches.

"It is really quite easy, Miss Melville," Mr. Thespidos said briskly, as if he knew he had won the battle. "You will go to-morrow to Lord Warburton's house, which I have already ascertained is only fifteen miles from here and where he is at this moment in residence."

Corena parted her lips to tell him she could not do such a thing.

Then she was aware that, whatever she said, Mr. Thespidos would override it.

"You will tell Lord Warburton what I have told you to say and plead with him, if necessary on bended knees, to take you to Greece."

"And . . . if he . . . refuses?"

"I have already told you," Mr. Thespidos said in an oily voice, "that you resemble Aphrodite!"

"But the Aphrodite in which His Lordship is interested was made of marble!" Corena said scathingly. "I doubt if he would be interested in a living version."

"In which case your father will remain where he is— until we find him an encumbrance!"

This was plain speaking, and only with a supreme effort did Corena prevent herself from screaming.

Instead, she turned round towards the mantelpiece to stand with her back to Mr. Thespidos.

She could hardly believe what she had just heard was not some terrible nightmare from which she would wake up to find it was all untrue.

How could her father, who was so intelligent, find himself in the clutches of this horrible man who was threatening her?

He was, she knew, evil and avaricious, and undoubtedly one of the Greeks of whom her father had spoken.

They were only interested in the statues and treasures to be found amongst the ruins for what they personally could get out of them.

The only thing to do, she thought suddenly, was to tell Lord Warburton the whole truth.

Again, as if Mr. Thespidos knew what she was thinking, he said quietly:

"If you do anything but what I have told you to do, Miss Melville, we might find it incumbent upon us to torture your father a little further in case he has information he has not yet divulged to us, and then, when there is no more to learn, dispose of him."

Corena turned round.

"What you are planning is a wicked and criminal act!" she said. "I have always respected the Greeks, but you are a charlatan and a murderer!"

She spoke in a low voice.

Yet every word she spoke was like a dagger she threw at the man she hated.

Mr. Thespidos listened, then he laughed, and the sound seemed to echo round the room.

"Magnificent!" he approved. "You look even more beautiful when you are angry! What could be more awe-inspiring than a goddess declaiming in a divine rage against a man who will not listen to her?"

Because she hated him so intensely, Corena turned back towards the mantelpiece.

There was silence, until she said in a different tone:

"If I . . . try to do as . . . you ask, will you . . . swear to me that in the . . . meantime you will not . . . hurt my father?"

"That is better!" Mr. Thespidos said. "Now we can talk business!"

She reluctantly turned again to face him.

"What you have to do, Miss Melville," he said, "is to carry out my orders, and as soon as Lord Warburton tells you when he will be leaving for Greece, you will inform the man whom I will leave here."

He paused for a moment to look at her calculatingly before he said:

"From that moment you can relax and leave everything in my hands."

"That . . . is what . . . horrifies me!" Corena said with a flash of spirit.

Mr. Thespidos smiled.

"You will get everything you want: your father returned to you in good health. And from the time the yacht sets sail from Folkestone harbour, where it is at this moment, I give you my word, he will not be touched."

Corena drew in her breath and Mr. Thespidos went on:

"If, on the other hand, you were so foolish as to inform Lord Warburton what has passed between us and he should telegraph the authorities in Athens, then I am afraid, Miss Melville, you will never see your father again!"

"I cannot believe this is true!" Corena cried. "I cannot believe there are men like you in what is otherwise a very beautiful and happy world!"

"That is what you have found, Miss Melville," Mr. Thespidos said sarcastically, "but other people are hungry, other people need money! You must therefore learn to share your happiness or, at least, pay for it."

"What I am . . . concerned with is . . . my father's . . . safety!"

Mr. Thespidos rose to his feet and gave a gesture that was entirely Greek.

"That is up to you," he said, "and I have the feeling that you will prove to be a competent and exceedingly sensible young woman."

His voice sharpened, and once again Corena was conscious of how evil he was as he added:

"As I have already said, on your knees, or in His Lordship's bed, is the only possible way by which you can save your father!"

Corena gave a little gasp.

Never in the whole of her quiet and sheltered life had anyone spoken to her in such an outrageous manner.

She wanted to scream abuse at the Greek, but she knew it would only be a waste of words and also undignified.

Instead, she said:

"You have left me no choice but to try to save my father's life, and I can only pray that, criminal though you are, you will keep your word!"

Mr. Thespidos laughed.

"I like your spirit, Miss Melville," he said. "I can assure you that once Lord Warburton is in our hands your father will be in yours, and if you are wise, you will take him back to England and persuade him to stay here!"

Now his tone was not only menacing, but at the same time dominating and aggressive because he had got his own way.

Corena was also aware of the way he was looking at her, and the expression in his eyes made her feel sick.

With a pride of which she knew her father would have approved, she merely said:

"Good-day, Mr. Thespidos. I presume the man who is waiting to hear when Lord Warburton will be leaving for Greece will also inform me how I can get in touch with you once we reach your country."

"I have already told you, Miss Melville, to leave everything in my hands," Mr. Thespidos replied. "They are very capable, and at the same time I never relinquish my grip."

He was threatening her again.

As if she could bear no more, Corena turned round with her back towards him and said again:

"Good-day, Mr. Thespidos!"

She heard him rise to his feet.

She felt as if his eyes were burning their way penetratingly into her body.

She was not certain what he was thinking—at the same time she was suddenly afraid of him in a different way than she had been before.

Then he made a murmur, almost as if he spoke to himself.

He turned and she heard him walk lightly across the room towards the door.

When he reached it, she knew he looked back.

But only when she heard the door close and his footsteps going across the marble hall did she put her hands up to her face.

She was not crying, she was just stricken with the horror of the situation.

She was afraid, desperately, terrifyingly afraid for her father and the future.

chapter two

LORD Warburton walked ahead into his study.

It was one of the most attractive rooms in the house and had a magnificent view over the garden.

Its sporting pictures were some of the finest ever painted by Stubbs and Sartorius.

The chairs were upholstered in red leather, and so was the fireguard, which had a cushioned seat.

Lord Warburton sat down on it and said to his friend as he advanced towards him:

"You are looking well, Charles, but rather thin."

"It is not surprising," Major Charles Bruton replied, "considering I have been exercising your horses from the crack of dawn until dusk."

"What do you think of them?"

"Absolutely superb! Especially those with a touch of Arab in them!"

Lord Warburton smiled slightly.

It removed for an instant the cynical look which characterised his face.

"Then I hope we shall win a number of races with them," he said dryly.

"I am prepared to bet on that!" Charles Bruton replied.

"Unfortunately, I shall not be here to see them run."

Charles Bruton, who was seating himself in one of the comfortable armchairs, looked at him in surprise and exclaimed:

"You are surely not going to Greece again!"

"I have to!"

"Why?"

"Because I have heard of something extraordinary which is what I have been looking for for a long time, and I dare not miss the opportunity of acquiring it."

Charles Bruton sighed.

"I would have thought, Orion, you had enough Greek statuary to fill a museum!"

"Can one ever have enough of a good thing?" Lord Warburton asked. "I might say the same about horses!"

His friend Charles laughed.

He had left the Army with the reputation of being the best rider in the Household Cavalry.

Lord Warburton, realising he was hard-up, had offered him the position of Manager of his racing-stable.

Charles Bruton had jumped at the chance.

It was not only the present Lord Warburton who had built up the stable, but his father and his grandfather before him, with the result that horses carrying the Warburton colours which ran in every Classic race had now become a legend.

"I must say," Charles remarked now, "I think it rather

shabby of you, after all my hard work, not to be in at the finish."

"I am sorry, Charles, and I knew you would be disappointed," Lord Warburton replied, "but as you know, when it is a question of a contest, Greece comes first!"

"I suppose I should have expected that," Charles Bruton said, "and this particular object which is taking you away from England, is it really better than what you have already?"

"I cannot answer that question until I have seen it," Lord Warburton answered, "but my informant, who has helped me before, has written to me very positively to say that this is something unique and if I miss it, I will regret it for ever."

"What is it?" Charles enquired.

"It is a statue of Aphrodite which Archaeologists have been seeking for years, and which so far has eluded the French, the Germans, and before them the Romans."

"I should have thought Aphrodite, the Goddess of Love, was very inappropriate for you!"

"Not if she is made of marble," Lord Warburton replied.

"I must admit I would feel much happier," Charles said, "if you had told me you were going to Paris to search for an Aphrodite made of flesh and blood. As you well know, it is something you should be doing."

"What do you mean—I *should* be doing?"

"Do not be obtuse, Orion," his friend replied. "You know as well as I do that you have to get married sooner or later and produce an heir. What, otherwise, is to happen to all this?"

He threw out his arms in a gesture as he spoke.

It embraced the magnificent pictures and two exceptional statues that stood one on either side of the fire-place.

They were both of men, naked in the characteristic athletic pose, with the victor's ribbon in their hair.

Lord Warburton did not answer for a moment.

Then he said:

"You have said this to me before, but there is plenty of time."

"At thirty-two, if you get much older, it will be impossible for you to marry a young and beautiful Aphrodite, and you will have to make do with a widow who will undoubtedly be only too eager to marry you for your wealth and position."

Lord Warburton laughed.

"A gloomy picture! But I am not convinced that a gauche young woman without a brain in her head would be any better!"

Charles stretched out his legs and lay back in his chair, scrutinising his friend.

"You worry me," he said. "For the last two years you have grown more and more cynical, and it seems impossible for any woman, however attractive she may be, to hold your attention."

He thought Lord Warburton would laugh.

Instead, he rose from the fire-stool and walked restlessly across the room.

He stood at the window, looking out at the green lawns sloping down to the lake, at the far side of which was an exquisite white temple he had brought back from Greece.

Charles waited, and after a definite pause Lord Warburton said:

"The truth is, I find women—all women—disappointing!"

"That is impossible!" Charles expostulated.

"It is true," Lord Warburton replied. "They may look lovely, but as soon as I get to know them, I find them stupid, trivial, and in many ways uncivilised."

"I think you must be mad!"

"No, I am sane, and I find it so much easier to talk to men older than myself who have lived their lives fully, or else are interested in the glories of the past."

"Especially those of Greece!" Charles Bruton said beneath his breath.

"Yes, Greece!" Lord Warburton said firmly. "I only wish to God I could have sat at the feet of Socrates and Plato, or listened to Homer, finding everything they said stimulating and exciting."

"But they are dead, and it is ridiculous for you, of all people, to spend your time in longing for the unattainable and searching for dead bones."

"What is the alternative?" Lord Warburton asked. "To dance attendance on the ageing Prince of Wales, to listen to those who surround the Queen, drooling on about the Empire?"

"London has other attractions."

"By which you mean," Lord Warburton said mockingly, "that I should be obsessed by the Gaiety Girls and think myself privileged to take one of them to supper? Good God, Charles, have you ever talked to one of those much-extolled 'Beauties' of the Gaiety?"

"Of course I have," Charles replied, "and have found them very amusing!"

"To drink champagne out of a silk slipper and drive them home in a hansom cab when dawn breaks?" Lord Warburton asked sarcastically.

"I can think of more intimate pleasures," Charles murmured.

"On those occasions," Lord Warburton replied, "one does not have to listen, or talk!"

Charles laughed.

"All right, Orion, you win! Go to Greece, find your Aphrodite! All I can say is that marble is very cold in bed and stone lips are not particularly responsive!"

Lord Warburton did not answer. He only walked back to where he had been sitting before.

Then in a different tone of voice he said:

"Now let us talk, and I want to hear every detail about my horses before I leave."

Charles obliged him.

At the same time, he could not help thinking that despite all his great possessions, his friend was not a particularly happy man.

He had admired Orion ever since they were together at Eton.

They had then gone on to Oxford.

Charles had concentrated on sport and the companionship of those who enjoyed the same pursuits as he did.

Orion, however, had taken a degree in Archaeology.

He was acclaimed as being the best student of Oriental languages that Oxford had ever produced.

However, they remained friends.

When they went into the Life Guards together, Charles was still admiring a man who could ride better and look more handsome than anybody else in the Regiment.

Then they had served together in India as Aides-de-camp to the Viceroy.

Charles knew that on several occasions Orion had been in dangerous situations.

He survived only by the quickness of his brain and an

intuition which at times could be uncannily perceptive.

When they returned to England Orion had come into the title, and having left the Regiment was concerned with his estates.

For the following year the friends saw very little of each other.

Then Charles took over the Warburton racing-stable.

Now, whenever his employer was in England they were together most of the time.

Charles was worried because Orion seemed to get so little pleasure out of life, except when he was in Greece.

He would be excited only when he brought back to Warburton Park the treasures from his last journey.

Charles enjoyed a pleasant succession of passionate love-affairs.

He found it hard to believe that his friend was happy without the delight of having a soft, warm body in his arms, and eager lips seeking his.

Yet Lord Warburton appeared to be immune to the women who pursued him relentlessly.

He found any woman's attractions palled after a short space of time.

Charles was aware that he had been disillusioned when he was very young during his first year at Oxford.

It had been, he had thought at the time, quite unimportant.

Looking back, he was certain it was from that moment that his friend had seemed to avoid women.

Alternatively, when he was with them, he regarded them cynically.

He could understand that it was difficult for any woman, especially one with an ambitious mother, not to be aware that he was a tremendous "catch," apart from being an extremely handsome and attractive man.

Charles, who found all women were like beautiful flowers waiting for him to pick them, wanted his friend to enjoy their proximity as much as he did.

He found his preoccupation with what were, after all, only old pieces of marble inhuman and incomprehensible.

They had talked over the horses and Charles had told him which races he hoped they would win.

Then he said pleadingly:

"Why do you not change your mind, Orion? Forget Greece for the moment and come and watch your colours first past the winning-post at Newmarket, and, of course, at Royal Ascot."

"I would like to do that," Lord Warburton admitted, "but if I lose Aphrodite, I may never have such an opportunity again!"

"There are some very pretty 'Aphrodites' in London," Charles said temptingly, "one in particular whom I have been wanting you to meet for some time."

"I will meet her when I return, and if she is more beautiful than the Aphrodite I expect to bring back with me, perhaps I will marry her!"

Charles laughed. Then he said seriously:

"I hope you will do that, for actually she would make a very suitable wife, although she might find it somewhat irksome to have to share your affections with a lot of women made of marble, beautiful though they may be!"

"If you are suggesting that to marry her I shall have to move my goddesses into a museum or create one in the West Wing," Lord Warburton said, "then I shall refuse categorically to walk up the aisle!"

Charles was about to make some flippant retort, then thought it would be a mistake.

He realised how proud his friend was of his Grecian antiquities.

To suggest that any woman who married him might sweep away the lot would, he was quite certain, preclude his ever "popping the question."

'I must be tactful about this,' he thought.

Instead, he said:

"Very well, Orion, go to Greece and collect your Aphrodite! Then, as you have promised, when you come home, seek for a goddess young and alive who will make your heart beat faster, and will provide you with half-a-dozen sons as handsome as you are yourself!"

Lord Warburton laughed, but it was a little wryly.

Charles was not the only person who was always begging him to marry.

He thought irritably that his relations talked of little else.

He knew only too well that they all disliked his heir-presumptive, a cousin who was already middle-aged.

He had, however, an unquenchable hope that he would somehow step into his shoes.

It was he who was the most effusive about his collection for the simple reason that he hoped Lord Warburton would encounter some fatal danger on his journeys to the Mediterranean.

Perhaps Lord Warburton's yacht would sink and he would be drowned in a storm in the Bay of Biscay.

Lord Warburton, who was well aware of other people's feelings, knew what his cousin was hoping and praying would happen.

He felt more determined for that reason, if nothing else, to keep alive.

At the same time, he was honest enough to know that sooner or later he must marry.

He would produce the longed-for heir to the title, although the idea appalled him.

Charles was right in thinking he had been disillusioned.

He could still remember the way the girl he had admired and whom he was attracted to had laughed at his interest in Greece.

She had sneered at the poems he found so beautiful and at the statues he took her to see in the British Museum.

The "Elgin Marbles" had thrilled him ever since he had seen them when he was quite small.

On his first vacation from Oxford he had gone to Paris to see the Grecian statues in the Louvre and the sculptures in Munich.

Because they meant so much to him, he had brought back for the girl drawings and photographs of what had thrilled him.

She told him scathingly that she would have preferred a piece of jewellery and had no interest in "that old rubbish!"

At first he could hardly credit what she was saying.

Then, as she sneered at his absorption in what to him was almost sacred, he learned that the poems he had written her in the Grecian style had been the cause of much laughter.

She had shown them and ridiculed them not only to her own friends, but to his, and he told himself he would never again be deceived by a pretty face.

There had been many women intermittently in his life.

It had been impossible to avoid them when he was so good-looking and so distinguished.

They had, however, never meant more to him then a physical enjoyment.

It was much as a man enjoys a good meal, then forgets it immediately it is finished.

He was well aware that even his friend Charles did not completely understand the beauty he found in Greece.

The statues thrilled him as no woman had ever been able to do.

At the same time, they stimulated his mind and lifted his whole being towards the light of the stars.

Because his mother had been a great lover of poetry, she had christened him Orion.

In deference to the family tradition, his other names were George Frederick.

It was only when he was old enough to decide such things for himself that he dropped his first two names.

He insisted on using the one which was Greek.

Because he looked so romantic, people thought it appropriate, and there were few of his friends except Charles brave enough to tease him about it.

The two men were still talking animatedly when the door of the Study opened.

"Excuse me, M'Lord," the Butler, who had been at the Park for over thirty years, said apologetically, "but there's a young lady here who insists on seeing Your Lordship."

"What does she want, McGregor?" Lord Warburton asked.

"She asked if you'll see her, M'Lord, and says it's a matter of life and death!"

Lord Warburton looked surprised, and Charles Bruton laughed.

"That is certainly a change from the Vicar begging for a contribution towards the Orphanage!"

"I suppose I had better see her," Lord Warburton said a little wearily.

He was aware as soon as he had come to live at the Park that there was always somebody to bore him with their complaints or to ask for money for some local charity.

"I've shown the young lady into the Silver Salon, M'Lord."

"Very well," Lord Warburton said, "I will join her there."

"A matter of life and death!" Charles said as the Butler closed the door. "It sounds exciting!"

"I doubt it," Lord Warburton replied. "My guess is that it is a collection for a Missionary in Africa. They are always requiring funds to convert the natives, who much prefer their own religions."

"You are not only cynical," Charles said accusingly, "but unromantic. I can think of much better reasons for a young woman to call on you."

Lord Warburton was, however, walking towards the door.

"If I am too long," he said, "come and rescue me."

"Very well," Charles answered, "but if she is pretty, it would not hurt you give her a fiver."

He was not certain Lord Warburton heard the last words.

He had shut the door before he finished speaking.

Then, as Charles picked up the newspapers, he felt what a pity it was that his friend could not find somebody who attracted him as much as the Aphrodite he was seeking in Greece.

'If she were alive now,' Charles thought, 'Orion would doubtless find her a prosaic bore. It is only because she is unattainable that he continues to search for what he will never find.'

He sighed and, picking up a newspaper, turned to the sporting page.

*   *   *

Corena had woken in the morning feeling what had happened the day before must have been a dream.

And yet, when she remembered the Greek's dark eyes and the way in which he had spoken, she knew it was only too real.

To save her father she had to visit Lord Warburton.

She could hardly credit even to herself that she was faced with such a dilemma.

The horror of it made her sit up in bed shivering although the warm sun was streaming through the drawn-back curtains.

She had not told her old Governess, Miss Davis, last night about her visitor.

Nor did she intend to inform her of where she was going to-day.

Although Miss Davis had a keen intelligence, Corena felt that she would never understand.

Whatever it might cost her personally, she had to save her father's life.

Somehow it was impossible to believe that if she did not follow his instructions, Mr. Thespidos would actually murder him.

"How can there be men like that in the world?" she asked herself despairingly.

She got out of bed and began to dress.

She had the uncomfortable feeling that what Mr. Thespidos had said was no idle threat, and if she did not do as he said, she would never see her father again.

The whole thing was so terrifying that she felt herself praying to her mother for help.

She felt like a child who runs instinctively when there is danger to its parent, where it will find security.

She wondered if there was anyone she could contact and explain the position she was in.

She thought it unlikely they would believe her.

What was more, Mr. Thespidos had not left her an address.

There was no way she could contact him.

The only person who knew where he was was the man he had left waiting to hear the result of her visit to Lord Warburton.

Finally, because there was nothing else she could do, she ordered the carriage.

Drawn by two horses, it was to be brought round to the front-door in half-an-hour's time.

As her maid hurried downstairs to obey her instructions, she stood at her wardrobe wondering what she should wear.

The weather was very warm for the beginning of May.

She looked at a pretty gown that she had brought recently to please her father.

It was well cut, with a skirt swelling out from her tiny waist.

Then she remembered Mr. Thespidos had said that the only possible way she could save her father was "on her knees or in His Lordship's bed."

She had been shocked at the time, and even more

shocked when at night she thought over what Mr. Thespidos had implied.

She was very innocent and completely unsophisticated because she had lived such a quiet life in the country.

Corena was aware that men did have illicit relationships with women, but she had little idea of what this entailed.

She knew only that it was wrong and wicked, something that her mother never discussed with her, or her father mentioned.

Because they were so happy together, Corena had always believed that one day she would find a man as attractive and intelligent as her father.

They would fall in love with each other.

They would be married.

They would share a common interest in Greece, in their horses, and in their children.

It all seemed as beautiful as the first spring daffodils golden under the trees, the ducklings swimming behind their mothers on the lake, the white doves flying over the house against the blue of the summer sky.

She knew it was a beauty which tugged at her heart, the beauty she found everywhere in her home.

She thought one day she would find it in love.

Hastily, because Mr. Thespidos seemed to be whispering the words in her ears, she took from the wardrobe a gown she had never liked.

She had bought the material for it by artificial light and in the daytime it looked drab and rather dowdy.

She put it on and covered the fair gold of her hair with a bonnet that she wore only at funerals.

She added to it a small veil which had belonged to her mother.

She looked at herself in the mirror, then, still afraid of what she could see, she went to her father's room.

In a small drawer in his chest-of-drawers she found what she sought.

It was a pair of spectacles he usually took with him when he went abroad.

He had left them behind this time because one of the lenses had a crack in it.

He had, therefore, bought another pair.

Corena had had this pair repaired and left in the drawer to await his return.

They were slightly tinted.

They obscured the beauty of Corena's eyes and the gold specks which looked like sunshine on clear water.

She put the spectacles into her hand-bag.

When she was told that the carriage was at the door, she went downstairs.

Because they needed exercise, the horses were fidgeting and tossing their heads, with their long manes.

For a second she thought she must be mad to obey Mr. Thespidos.

How could she supplicate a man she had never met and whom she was afraid would refuse her request.

'I have to persuade him!' she thought.

Then once again Mr. Thespidos's words made her shudder.

She had told Miss Davis the night before that she was going out early.

The old Governess had replied:

"In which case, dear, I think I will spend the morning in bed. I have not been sleeping well lately and it will do me good to relax."

"Yes, of course," Corena agreed. "I will tell them to

send your luncheon up on a tray, but I should be back by tea-time."

"I will be downstairs by then," Miss Davis promised, "and thank you, dear child, for being so understanding."

Corena had gone from the room knowing that what she had to accept was that Miss David was growing very old.

She felt a little tremor at the thought that perhaps she might die.

She would have to find somebody else to be with her when her father was away.

But this morning she could concentrate only on her main problem, which was Lord Warburton.

As the carriage carried her away, she tried to plan what she would say to him.

She had to make it sound convincing.

She had to make him feel that he must, at whatever inconvenience to himself, take her with him to Greece.

Then she began to wonder how Mr. Thespidos was aware of what Lord Warburton would be seeking in Greece.

He was also so knowledgeable about everything that concerned his household.

She had the suspicion that his informant must be one of His Lordship's servants.

She was sure that Mr. Thespidos would not hesitate to bribe any servant, whoever they belonged to, if it suited his purpose.

The mere thought of the Greek made her tremble.

She knew she was afraid of a man for the first time in her life.

It was an unpleasant feeling, and one she had never expected to experience.

He had a hard expression in his eyes and a cruelty

she now recognized from the thin line of his lips.

They gave her sensations she had never encountered before.

"I hate him! I hate him!" she told herself.

She drove on.

She did not see the green buds in the hedgerows, the primroses growing in the grass, or hear the cuckoos calling in the trees.

Usually she would have been entranced by the blue of the sky as it was reflected in the small streams they passed.

There was so much to see in the countryside, but Corena was thinking of her father.

He was imprisoned in a house, or perhaps only a small hut, somewhere in Greece.

Her whole being went out to him.

"I will . . . save you . . . Papa . . . I will . . . save you!" she whispered beneath her breath.

She felt he would be aware of her prayers and her love for him.

It was fifteen miles to Lord Warburton's house.

It was just after twelve o'clock when Corena saw ahead of her a huge mansion standing near a lake with a wood of fir trees behind it.

There was no doubt that Warburton Park was extremely impressive.

With the sun shining on its hundreds of windows and Lord Warburton's standard flying on the roof, it was magnificent.

She drove down an avenue of ancient lime trees.

Just as they started on an incline to the lake, there was a sudden flight of white doves.

They settled on the green lawn near the lake.

It was so lovely, and at the same time ethereal, as if it came from another world.

Corena thought it must be a sign of good luck and her prayers had been heard.

Then insidiously, almost as if the devil were beside her, she heard Mr. Thespidos's words, and remembered her spectacles.

She took them out of her bag.

She adjusted them on her nose under the small veil she was wearing as the carriage drew up outside the door.

It took a little time to persuade the Butler that while she had no appointment, it was imperative she should see Lord Warburton.

Finally he had shown her into an attractive Salon.

The cornice was decorated with silver, as were the Ionic pillars supporting it.

The chandeliers, with their crystal glass, were also of silver, as were the fireguard, poker, and tongs.

The curtains were a soft shade of blue, and the same damask covered the chairs and the sofa.

There were on either side of the fireplace small tables which Corena knew had been made during the reign of Charles II.

Then, as she looked around, she saw in a half-dozen alcoves there were Grecian statues which would have thrilled her father.

They were outstandingly beautiful, and enhanced by the silver background of the alcove, their marble seemed to glimmer.

'If only Papa could see these!' Corena thought.

Then she remembered where she was, why she was here, and as she held her breath because it was so terrifying, the door opened.

41

As Lord Warburton walked into the room, Corena felt it was impossible to look at him.

She had the frightening feeling that he might be as unpleasant and perhaps as sensuous as Mr. Thespidos had been.

Then she heard him say:

"You wished to see me?"

She looked up and saw that he was tall, broad-shouldered, and in fact, the best-looking man she had ever seen in the whole of her life.

At the same time, she was immediately conscious that there was a dry note in his voice, as if he thought she was a nuisance.

What was more, the lines from his nose to his lips made him appear almost as if he were sneering at her.

She looked at him through her tinted spectacles.

She was aware, almost as if somebody had told her so, that he resented her intrusion.

Also, for some reason she could not ascertain, he despised her.

Quickly, because she was so nervous, she said in a voice that did not sound like her own:

"My name, My Lord, is Melville, and I have come to ask Your Lordship's help for my father, Sir Priam Melville."

She thought as she spoke that she sounded like a school-girl who was afraid of forgetting her lines.

She was not surprised when Lord Warburton replied:

"Suppose we sit down, Miss Melville, and you tell me why your father needs my help and has not come to ask for it personally."

Corena seated herself on the edge of the sofa.

Clasping her hands together in her lap, she said:

"My father is abroad . . . in fact he is in . . . Greece."

She saw Lord Warburton raise his eye-brows as if he were surprised, and she thought there was slightly more interest in his voice as he replied:

"In Greece? But I was told that you wished to see me because it was a matter of life and death."

"That is true, My Lord," Corena said. "My father is desperately ill, and I thought . . . as I heard you were going to Greece . . . you might be kind enough to take me with you."

Now Lord Warburton was definitely surprised, and he stared at her as if he could hardly believe what he had heard.

"I imagine, Miss Melville," he replied after a moment, "that you can travel to Greece in the customary manner by train."

"Trains are very . . . unpredictable . . . My Lord, especially in the . . . South of Europe," Corena replied. "That is why I thought if you could . . . possibly take me . . . with you . . . I could hope to reach Crisa far more surely than by any . . . other route."

"Then your father is at Delphi?"

"My father is an Archaeologist, as you are, but now he is very ill."

"Who told you this?"

"A man arrived yesterday from Greece to inform me that my father was . . . desperately ill but . . . receiving no . . . medical treatment."

She stumbled over the words, feeling, as she spoke, that they sounded foolish.

No one, least of all Lord Warburton, would believe her.

"You say that your father is an Archaeologist," Lord Warburton remarked, "but surely he is not alone while he is making his investigations?"

"My father usually works alone," Corena explained, "and he will never take a valet with him because he says English servants are often more trouble than they are worth in foreign countries."

She thought Lord Warburton smiled, but it was only a very faint twist of his lips before he replied:

"I appreciate that, Miss Melville. But I still think your best method of reaching your father is by train. I dare say, if you went first to Venice, you could find ships leaving almost daily for Greece."

"Please, My Lord . . . take me with . . . you?"

Corena felt there was nothing more she could say, except to plead with him.

For a moment there was silence. Then Lord Warburton replied:

"Are you saying, Miss Melville, that the reason you are so eager to travel with me is that you cannot afford the fare? In which case . . ."

With a sense of horror Corena realised he was going to offer her money, and she said hastily:

"No . . . no . . . it is not a . . . question of money . . . but of speed."

"As I have already explained to you, Miss Melville, it will be quicker by train. Although my yacht is new and capable of fourteen knots an hour, I can still be held up in a rough sea in the Bay of Biscay, and there are often storms which are time-consuming in the Mediterranean."

"I . . . I understand that, My Lord, but, please . . ."

Lord Warburton rose to his feet.

"I regret, of course, that I cannot be of assistance to you, and I can only promise you that if there is anything I can do once I reach Greece, I will if you get in touch with me."

It flashed through Corena's mind that if he told her when he was going and where his yacht would be anchored, that would perhaps content Mr. Thespidos.

"I thank Your Lordship for your . . . kindness," she said, "and if you will tell me where . . . you will be . . . it will be . . . comforting to know that if it is . . . impossible to get the sort of . . . help I need for my father, I shall be able to . . . contact you."

"I have an agent in Athens," Lord Warburton said, "and I will give you his address."

He walked across the room to where there was a beautifully inlaid French *secretaire*.

He took a piece of writing-paper from a leather holder embellished with his crest.

As he started to write, Corena's heart sank.

She knew that this would be useless, and she thought, too, that if Lord Warburton was being secretive about where he was going, he would not get in touch with his Agent or anybody else.

He walked back to where she was sitting and handed her the piece of paper.

"Here is the address, Miss Melville," he said, "and I can only hope when you reach Greece you will find your father is not as ill as you anticipate."

"You are . . . going to the . . . port of . . . Crisa?" Corena asked.

Almost as if Lord Warburton were aware she had a reason for asking the question, he replied:

"The one advantage of having a yacht, Miss Melville, is that one can go anywhere one pleases, without previous intention or even making plans."

"Yes . . . of course."

She put the piece of paper he handed her into her

bag, then, making one final effort to save her father from Mr. Thespidos, she said:

"Please . . . change your mind and . . . take me with you. I promise I will be no trouble . . . in fact you need not even be . . . aware that I am on board . . . but . . . I know it is the . . . best way to . . . reach my father."

"I am sorry to disappoint you, Miss Melville," Lord Warburton replied, "but my answer is 'No!'"

There was something firm and inflexible in the way he spoke.

She knew that even if, as Mr. Thespidos suggested, she went down on her knees, his answer would still be the same.

As if the subject were closed, Lord Warburton moved towards the door and there was nothing she could do but follow him.

He held it open for her and she stepped into the hall.

The front-door was open and there were footmen in Lord Warburton's livery on either side of it.

From the top of the steps Corena could see her carriage with its two horses waiting for her.

She thought despairingly that it might be a Funeral hearse.

In refusing her request, Lord Warburton was destroying her father and sending him to his death.

There was, however, nothing more she could say.

As they reached the door, he held out his hand.

"Good-bye, Miss Melville, and I hope your apprehension concerning your father will have proved to be unnecessary."

She put her hand lightly into his.

She had not replaced her glove, which she had taken off in the Silver Salon. She felt the warmth of his skin on her fingers.

Strangely, she felt some vibration from him.

She thought it was due to her agitation and his determination not to assist her.

Then, as she went down the steps towards the carriage, he did not wait to see her go.

She looked back and there was nobody at the open door.

The carriage drove away.

It was then she realised she had failed completely, and as she took off her spectacles, she wondered if it was her fault.

Perhaps she should have tried, as Mr. Thespidos had suggested, to entice him by her looks rather than by hesitating words.

His answer might then have been different.

'It is . . . too late . . . now,' she thought despairingly.

The horses' hoofs, as they started to quicken their pace up the drive, seemed to repeat the words over and over again:

"Too late! Too late!"

chapter three

CORENA arrived home.

She wondered apprehensively if there would be anybody waiting for her from Mr. Thespidos.

There appeared, however, to be nobody about.

She went upstairs to take off her hat and tidy her hair, and when she came down, everything seemed quiet.

She went into the Drawing-Room.

Through the open window she could hear the buzzing of the bees and the birds singing in the bushes.

She tried to believe that all this drama was only a nightmare.

But with a constriction of her heart she knew it was only too real.

Her father was in great danger, and entirely through her own fault she had failed to save him.

How could she have been so stupid as to go disguised in a pair of tinted spectacles.

Mr. Thespidos had suggested something vulgar and unpleasant, but what did it matter?

Was it likely for one moment that Lord Warburton who, from all she had heard was a man of great distinction, would notice somebody like herself, who was of no social consequence?

"I made a . . . mess of it . . . Mama!" she said in her heart.

She wondered if anyone could help her now.

She knew if her father died, she would always blame herself for having been so stupid.

She wondered whether, if she went back again and despite Mr. Thespidos's warning told Lord Warburton the truth, he would understand.

She knew that was a gamble which, if it failed, meant that her father would surely die.

It would be a great mistake to oppose Mr. Thespidos.

She was sure he was cruel and heartless, and would get his own way by hook or by crook.

"What . . . can I do? Oh . . . God, what can I . . . do?" she asked.

Because there was no answer to this, she could only pray.

She wandered restlessly from the house into the garden and back again as the hours passed slowly.

Then, when it was nearly four o'clock in the afternoon, she heard the sound of carriage wheels outside.

Just for one moment she wondered if by any chance Lord Warburton had changed his mind.

Had he come himself or sent someone to tell her so?

Then, as she realised this was an impossible idea, the door opened.

Bates, the old Butler said:

"A gentleman to see you, Miss Corena!"

Before she even looked, Corena knew who it was and felt herself shudder.

Mr. Thespidos walked slowly towards her.

He took, she thought, longer than necessary to reach her so that she would feel intimidated.

Her pride made her raise her chin, but she clasped her hands together.

She was trembling as she said before he could speak:

"I . . . I tried my best . . . but I am afraid . . . I failed!"

"I suppose it is what I might have expected," Mr. Thespidos said in what she thought was a disagreeable tone. "Now we have to put another plan into operation."

"Another . . . plan?" Corena asked.

"I presume you still wish to save your father's life?"

"Yes . . . of course! How can you . . . ask such a . . . thing?"

"Then you must do exactly as I tell you! Otherwise, make no mistake, Miss Melville, he will die, and it will not be a quiet or pleasant death!"

For a moment Corena thought she must scream at the horror of what he was saying.

Then, because something strong and resilient in her refused to allow the Greek to trample on her, she said:

"I have told you I will do anything I can to help my father, but I can see no point in indulging in threats and recriminations!"

There was a glint in Mr. Thespidos's eyes.

It told her that he was surprised at her air of defiance.

Then he said, and she thought a little more respectfully:

"I have thought out a way in which you can save your father and give me the information I require."

"What is . . . it?"

He looked at her speculatively, as if he were considering whether to tell her the truth or leave her in ignorance until the last minute.

Then because, she was sure, it amused him to frighten her, he said:

"You had your chance to solve this problem amicably, but you failed!"

"I am . . . aware of . . . that," Corena murmured.

"Now," Mr. Thespidos went on as if she had not spoken, "we will have to do something more drastic!"

"W-what are you . . . suggesting?"

He paused for a moment before he said slowly:

"You will be a stowaway on Lord Warburton's yacht!"

"A . . . stowaway?"

Whatever Corena was expecting, it was not this.

As she spoke, she stared at him in astonishment.

"When he finds you, or, rather, when you reveal yourself after it is too late for him to turn back, he will be forced to take you to Crisa, where I shall be waiting."

"B-but . . . such an idea is . . . impossible!" Corena protested.

There was a note of defiance in her voice which Mr. Thespidos did not miss.

"If he does discover me," she added quickly, "there is every . . . likelihood that he will . . . throw me out at . . . Gibraltar, or at one of the French ports if I am discovered earlier."

"In which case your father will die in a most unpleasant manner, which I imagine will haunt you for the rest of your life!"

Corena pressed her fingers together in an effort at self-control until they were bloodless.

Then she added in a voice that by a supreme effort was calm and slow:

"What are you . . . suggesting? How are you . . . planning that I shall . . . do this?"

"Now you are talking sense!" Mr. Thespidos said. "It would be polite, Miss Melville, if you would invite me to sit down."

Corena indicated a chair.

Then, because she felt her legs would not support her any longer, she sat down on a sofa.

She was finding it hard to breathe, hard to suppress the fear that was rising within her, and which she knew might at any minute overwhelm her.

"I have already worked out my plan," Mr. Thespidos said, "and I cannot find a flaw in it."

Corena waited, but he did not go on, and after a moment she asked:

"W-what . . . have you . . . decided?"

"I understand His Lordship will be leaving the day after tomorrow," Mr. Thespidos said, "and you will therefore be ready at nine o'clock to-morrow morning, when I will collect you."

"To go . . . where?"

"To travel to Folkestone, where His Lordship's yacht is in harbour. You will be aboard before he arrives."

"B-but . . . how? And when he . . . finds me there . . . surely he will refuse to . . . take me . . . with him?"

Mr. Thespidos smiled.

"You can leave everything in my hands, and all we have to do is to make arrangements to travel to the nearest station where we can pick up an Express."

He looked her over in a way she found repellent before he said:

"Bring your prettiest gowns with you, otherwise, if you are so foolish as to be put ashore and His Lordship goes on alone, you have only yourself to blame!"

What he insinuated was quite obvious, and Corena rose to her feet.

"Because I have no choice, Mr. Thespidos," she said, "I will be ready at the time you state . . . but I do not wish to . . . listen any more to your . . . insinuations as to how I should . . . behave. They are . . . repulsive and . . . extremely vulgar!"

She thought he might be slightly abashed by her retort, but instead he merely laughed.

"I can see you are a girl with spirit, Miss Melville!" he said. "If you drown, you will go down with all flags flying!"

Corena did not reply.

She just stood waiting for him to leave.

Once again he was appraising her with his eyes, making her feel almost as if he undressed her and left her naked.

"Nine o'clock, Miss Melville," he said, and, turning, walked from the room.

Corena did not cover her face as she had done the last time he left her.

Instead, she went to the open window as if in need of fresh air to counteract the way he had fouled the atmosphere.

"He is wicked, evil, cruel, and unscrupulous!" she said beneath her breath.

At the same time, she realised she was completely in his power, just as her father was.

There was nothing she could do, therefore, but obey him and carry out his plan, though she felt it was doomed to disaster.

How could he possibly get her aboard Lord Warburton's yacht without the crew being aware of it?

If he tried to hide her in some corner of it under cover of darkness, it was an attempt that was utterly impractical.

She could think of a thousand reasons that Mr. Thespidos's plan of smuggling her aboard was bound to fail.

She wished now she had argued with him further.

Then she knew that to be near to him made her feel a revulsion which stupefied her brain.

She realised that she had no option but to obey him.

She went upstairs to her bed-room.

It made her shudder to think of his purpose in telling her to pack her prettiest gowns to take with her.

She put a number of them on the bed.

Then she rang for a housemaid to tell her they were to be packed immediately.

"You're goin' away, Miss?" the maid enquired.

"I am afraid so," Corena replied, "but I do not think it will be for long."

Mr. Thespidos's ridiculous plan would, she was sure, result in her being exposed long before the yacht left harbour.

Then she remembered that, if that happened, her father would be murdered.

She felt the horror of it so intensely that it was impossible to say any more.

She sat in her bed-room until she had composed herself.

Then she went in search of Miss Davis.

She had already seen her before luncheon, and realised that she was not at all well.

"I shall be all right in a day or two," Miss Davis had said vaguely. "I get these attacks, and there's nothing to be done about it."

"Would you like me to send for a doctor?" Corena enquired.

Miss Davis had smiled.

"I have had him before, and he could do nothing. I think it is just something wrong with my intestines, and it will clear up within a few days—it always does!"

"You are very brave."

"I have found in life there is not much alternative," Miss Davis replied, "and sooner or later we all reach the end. At my age I try to keep my self-respect."

Corena bent forward to kiss her old Governess on the cheek.

"You have taught me to be brave too," she said, and knew it was the truth.

As she walked along to Miss Davis's room now, she knew she was showing courage in not burdening the old woman with her troubles.

She would have liked to consult Miss Davis.

She had a sharp, intelligent brain, and might, although it seemed impossible, find a way out of this terrible *impasse*.

But Corena knew it would shock and upset her to know of the alternative to doing what Mr. Thespidos had ordered her to do.

What was more, if she did go through with it and did not return immediately from Folkestone, Miss Davis would worry herself almost into the grave.

"If she can be brave, I can be brave by keeping my mouth shut," Corena decided.

As she reached Miss Davis's room, she said:

"As you are not feeling well, I am going away with a friend for a few days. It will give you a chance to rest, and when I come back I know you will be on your feet again."

"That is a sensible thing to do," Miss Davis approved, "and the change will do you good. I thought this morning you were looking a little pale."

That was not surprising, Corena thought.

She had been awake practically the whole night worrying about her father and her interview with Lord Warburton.

"I am going to pack now," she said, feeling it would be a mistake to allow Miss Davis to ask too many questions, "but, of course, I will come and say good-night to you."

"Take your prettiest gowns, dear," Miss Davis said. "You might meet a charming young Romeo!"

This was an old joke, as there were few attractive men in the locality.

With an effort Corena managed to smile before she replied:

"One never knows!"

As she returned to her own bed-room she was thinking in horror of Mr. Thespidos, and with apprehension of Lord Warburton.

She knew if she was stowed away and he discovered her, they would have an extremely unpleasant interview.

She had the feeling that he would be very frightening if he was angry.

She was not frightened of him in the same way that she was frightened of Mr. Thespidos, which was a very different thing.

Yet because he was a very important and masculine

man, he made her feel small, insignificant, and completely inadequate.

"Which is what I am!" Corena told herself. "I suppose, if I were really intelligent, I would go to London to see the Secretary of State for Foreign Affairs and ask him to save Papa."

Then she knew without being told that this would take time.

What was more, no one knew where Mr. Thespidos had hidden her father.

'If I approached the Secretary of State, I am sure he would contact either the Police or the Military in Athens, which might be the right thing to do,' she thought.

Then something told her that Mr. Thespidos would be clever enough to avoid being arrested.

As her father was his prisoner, he would be killed.

Alternatively, he could be left to starve before they could find out where he was hidden.

'I can do only . . . what I have been . . . told to . . . do,' Corena thought despairingly.

She got into bed and knew that she was in for another sleepless night.

*   *   *

Corena was waiting downstairs in the hall.

Punctually at nine o'clock Mr. Thespidos arrived in an expensive-looking carriage drawn by two horses.

He did not waste time in getting out to greet her politely, so she hurried down the steps towards him.

Bates opened the carriage-door and she stepped inside while her luggage was strapped onto the back.

"'Ave a nice time, Miss Corena!" Bates said in a

fatherly manner. "I'll look after everythin' while you're away."

"I know you will, Bates, and I hope to be back soon."

As they drove away she sat back on the carriage-seat, moving as far away as possible from Mr. Thespidos.

She thought there was a smug smile of satisfaction on his lips.

After quickly glancing at him, she looked away because the mere sight of him made her feel sick.

"I hate him! I hate him!" she found herself saying silently.

It took them about an hour to reach the Railway Junction where Mr. Thespidos knew they could pick up a train from London which would go directly to Folkestone.

While he had taken First Class tickets, fortunately they did not have a reserved carriage.

There were two other people in their carriage.

Although one was an elderly gentleman who slept most of the way, it prevented Corena from having to make conversation with Mr. Thespidos who sat opposite her.

As she looked out of the window she could feel his eyes staring at her in a way she greatly disliked.

After a time, although she had no wish to read, she opened the newspaper she had bought at the station, and held it so that he was unable to see anything but the top of her hat.

Their luncheon was brought to them by a white-coated steward.

Although Corena ate a little of it, she felt as if she were swallowing sawdust and had no idea what anything she put in her mouth really tasted like.

To her relief, Mr. Thespidos fell asleep immediately after luncheon.

She thought in repose his face looked even more repulsive than it did when he was awake.

His features were coarse and not in the least what she expected of a Greek.

His skin was swarthy, and there were a number of pock-marks which told her that he had suffered from smallpox when he was young.

There was no doubt that every line of his face was cruel and hard.

She saw, too, that without the brightness of his shrewd, calculating eyes, there were lines on his face which made him look older than she had thought him to be at first.

However, she tried not to think about Mr. Thespidos, even though he was sitting opposite her.

She sent out her love and thoughts to her father.

She felt somehow that he must know how worried she was about him, and how she was trying to save him even though it might be impossible.

If only she could talk it over with him, she was sure he would find a solution.

But as it was, there was nothing she could do but pray and believe that God would somehow help her.

* * *

Mr. Thespidos woke up as the train neared Folkestone and said in a bright tone:

"Now the adventure begins! If you were a man, you would be excited by the thought!"

"Unfortunately I am a woman!" Corena replied.

"Meaning, I suppose," he said, "that if you were a

man, you would manhandle me until I told you what you wanted to know."

Corena was about to make some reply.

Then she realised that the middle-aged woman on the other side of the carriage who was travelling with the old man was looking at her with curiosity.

Without replying, she merely stared out the window until the train ran into the station.

Mr. Thespidos, giving orders in what Corena thought was a rude and unpleasant manner, collected her luggage from the Guard's Van.

They were met at the barrier by a man who greeted Mr. Thespidos respectfully.

Corena decided he was a clerk.

"Is everything arranged?" Mr. Thespidos enquired, and now he was speaking in Greek.

"It is as you ordered, Sir," the man replied.

Corena could understand, because her father had taught her to speak modern Greek when she was a small child.

She also knew a little, but not much, of the ancient Greek that he could read fluently.

He frequently translated for her so that she could enjoy the Odes of Pindar and the Plays of Sophocles.

She wisely, however, gave them no hint that she could understand what they were saying.

Perhaps by some miracle, she thought, she could learn something about her father, the most important being where they held him imprisoned.

A carriage was waiting for them outside the station.

Mr. Thespidos and Corena got inside while the man who had come to meet them sat on the box beside the coachman to show him the way.

She was sure that when they left the broad streets of

the town they were going towards the harbour.

Corena was wondering what Mr. Thespidos intended to do.

It was hardly possible that he meant to smuggle her aboard the yacht in daylight.

She was sure there would be seamen moving about.

The carriage came to a standstill and she realised they were outside one of the large buildings on the wharf.

The other Greek man climbed down from the box to open the door, and he helped Corena to alight.

Then they waited outside the door of what appeared to be an uninhabited building for Mr. Thespidos to produce a key.

The door opened and the younger man went ahead.

Corena followed Mr. Thespidos, who entered in front of her without apology.

There was just enough light from a window high up on the wall for Corena to see that they were moving along a narrow passage.

Now there were some stairs, and as they climbed up them the Greek ahead lit an oil-lamp which was on the landing.

He picked it up to light their way.

Mr. Thespidos walked into what Corena saw was an office.

It was then she realised that they were in a storage wharf with an office on the first floor which was surprisingly well-furnished.

There was a thick carpet on the floor and a large, imposing-looking desk.

A number of filing-cabinets covered one wall and two armchairs and a leather-covered sofa furnished the room.

The Greek put down the lamp on the desk, then descended the stairs.

He returned a few minutes later with Corena's trunk.

He put it down beside the door and obviously waited for further orders.

"You have procured what I told you?" Mr. Thespidos asked, again speaking Greek.

"Yes, Sir, it is downstairs."

"Then bring it up! I want Miss Melville to see it."

The Greek man disappeared and Mr. Thespidos, pulling off his coat and hat, said sharply:

"You might as well make yourself comfortable. We are staying here until dawn to-morrow morning."

"I would like to know what you are planning," Corena replied. "It was impossible to . . . speak on the train, but now we are alone and I . . . dislike being . . . kept in ignorance."

"Then I will show you," Mr. Thespidos said.

He walked towards the door as he spoke and she could hear the Greek man coming slowly up the stairs.

As he opened the door she saw that he carried in front of him what appeared to be a large packing-case.

She stared at it in astonishment, until in a voice that did not sound like her own she asked:

"Is . . . is that how you . . . intend to take me . . . on board the . . . yacht?"

"I knew you were an intelligent girl!" Mr. Thespidos replied. "Actually you will find it quite comfortable."

He opened the lid of the packing-case as he spoke.

Corena could see that it was padded inside with what appeared to be a coarse cotton material with something soft beneath it.

As she realised what he intended, she wanted to say

that she could not be shut in there and perhaps suffocate from lack of air.

He knew what she was thinking, and said:

"You will be able to breathe. We will drill holes along the top and sides, and you will be comfortable because this is how we bring very valuable cargo from Greece!"

From the way he spoke, Corena was suddenly aware that he traded in the priceless antiques that he had previously claimed belonged to his country.

He wanted to find out what her father and Lord Warburton were seeking simply so that he could sell it for a big price either in England or in Europe.

She would be taken aboard in the packing-case and Lord Warburton's staff would believe that it was part of his baggage.

It might, therefore, be a long time before he was even aware it was on board.

It was a clever idea, and she could see exactly how Mr. Thespidos's mind worked.

Once they were well away from English shores, Lord Warburton would feel almost obliged to take her to Crisa so that she could find her father.

She was thinking of this as she stood staring at the packing-case.

Only when she glanced at Mr. Thespidos again did she realise he had been watching her.

"Are you going to tell me how clever I am?" he asked in a mocking tone.

"I think it is a . . . horrible idea!" Corena cried. "Suppose nobody discovers where I am? I might die of starvation, if not from lack of air!"

"You underestimate me," Mr. Thespidos said complacently. "I have, of course, thought of that. There is a release catch in the box. It needs a little pressure on it, because otherwise it might open before you are ready to reveal yourself."

Quite suddenly Corena was frightened.

She felt to be shut up in a box and left to the mercy of a man who had already refused to help her was a fate so unpleasant that anything else might be preferable.

"Please . . ." she said, "I . . . I cannot do this . . . let me see Lord Warburton when he arrives . . . and plead with him once again to . . . take me as his . . . guest."

"And what if he refuses?" Mr. Thespidos asked.

He knew she had no answer to this, and he went on:

"No, I have made my plans and, you must admit, very cleverly. You will not be uncomfortable, and as you can let yourself out at any moment, there is no need to be afraid."

He smiled as he added:

"Think how pleased your father will be to see you!"

"You swear to me on everything you hold . . . sacred that I *shall* see my father when I . . . arrive?" Corena asked.

"The moment you give me Lord Warburton I shall have no further interest in your father," Mr. Thespidos said.

The way he spoke ought to have been reassuring.

Instead, there was something horrible in the way he spoke Lord Warburton's name, almost as if he mouthed over it.

Corena was certain that he was thinking of how much he would enjoy having anybody so important and so rich in his clutches.

Then she told herself she did not want to think about that. It was her father who concerned her.

She could not go on talking about it when the packing-case gaping at her from the floor made her tremble.

She moved back to the sofa, and Mr. Thespidos said to the man, addressing him as Paul:

"Take it downstairs and drill the air-holes as I told you to do. Four on each side of the box should be enough, and get a little more padding. We must make certain the lady is comfortable!"

He was speaking in English so that Corena could understand and he repeated it in Greek.

Paul picked up the packing-case and they could hear him going slowly down the stairs.

"There is a wash-room next door," Mr. Thespidos said, indicating a door, "and I suggest, after we have had something to eat that you rest on the sofa. The night will pass quicker if you sleep."

He did not sound particularly concerned about her comfort.

Corena wanted to say it would be impossible to sleep because of what lay ahead.

She knew, however, that it would be a mistake to bandy words with him.

Instead, she walked into the wash-room, hoping there would be a mirror so that she could tidy her hair when she took off her hat, and a basin in which she could wash her hands.

When she came back into the office it was to find that Mr. Thespidos was writing at his desk.

He had removed his coat and waist-coat so that he was sitting in his shirt-sleeves with his braces over his shoulders.

She thought it was very rude of him to treat her as if she were of no consequence, but there was nothing she could say.

Instead, she sat down on the sofa.

A few minutes later Paul arrived with a tray on which there was food for her to eat, although it was not particularly appetising.

At the same time, Corena felt she must keep up her strength.

She therefore forced herself to eat some of the cold meat and the salad which went with it.

She even accepted a glass of the Greek wine which Mr. Thespidos poured out for her.

One sip of it told her that it had a strong flavour of resin, and she refused to drink any more.

She asked, instead, for a glass of water.

Mr. Thespidos laughed and said:

"If you are going to stay in my country for any length of time, you will have to get used to the taste of our wines!"

He was mocking her.

She longed to reply that the sooner she was away from Greece and her father was safe, the better she would like it, but she thought it would be a mistake.

Instead, she went on eating, feeling the food was utterly tasteless because she was eating not for enjoyment, but simply to preserve her strength.

Mr. Thespidos, however, ate heartily, and drank most of the wine.

Then he said:

"Now we must settle down for the night, and I suppose you would not like me to kiss you good-night?"

Corena stiffened, but she decided it would be undignified to reply.

When he laughed she wondered frantically what she would do if he should attempt to touch her.

As if he knew what she was thinking, he said:

"You are quite safe. I have one motto in life and that

66

is 'Business First,' and to-morrow you will need your wits about you."

Corena continued with an effort to remain silent.

There was a cushion on the sofa to rest her head and there was a rug.

Paul had put it there when he came to take away their trays.

She lay down, having first taken off her shoes, and putting her head on the pillow, shut her eyes.

She knew that Mr. Thespidos was looking at her unpleasantly.

But she was sure he had spoken the truth when he had said that business came first.

From his point of view, if she was hysterical or too frightened, she might, after all, whatever the penalty, refuse to do what he asked of her.

She could hear him moving about the room before finally the makeshift bed at the other end of it creaked.

He turned out the lamp.

It was then, for the first time, that she relaxed a little, and when he began to snore, she knew she was safe.

In the darkness she began to pray passionately and desperately for help.

She was terrified of what the future might hold.

Yet she had the feeling that Lord Warburton, however angry he might be when he discovered her, was preferable to Mr. Thespidos.

She prayed for what seemed hours.

Then because she had not slept the night before, she fell into a hazy, dazed slumber in which she was half-thinking, half-dreaming, but not really asleep.

* * *

67

Corena was awoken by the sound of footsteps coming up the stairs. The door was opened and she heard Paul saying in Greek:

"It is half-past-five, Sir."

One more gigantic snore, and Mr. Thespidos woke up.

Before he could speak to her, Corena rose from the sofa and went into the wash-room.

She locked the door, washed her face and her hands, and tidied her hair.

She thought it would be unnecessary to put on her hat.

When she went out into the office she found Mr. Thespidos dressed in his waist-coat and tying the tie he must have removed before he slept.

"There is something for you to eat on my desk," he said as Corena re-entered, "and you had better eat it up. It may be a long time before you get anything more!"

This was common sense, although Corena resented the way he said it.

She found what was provided was bread, butter, and a hunk of cheese, and, to her relief, there was a pot of coffee.

She started to pour it out, then asked:

"There is only one cup. Do you not want some?"

"I will have some later," Mr. Thespidos replied, "once I have taken you aboard."

"How do you . . . know they will . . . accept me?"

"You leave that to me," he said, "I have got plenty of brains in my head."

She thought he leered at her as he spoke.

Having poured out her coffee, Corena forced herself to eat some of the bread, which was mercifully fresh,

68

and as much of the cheese as she could manage.

She wondered if she should suggest to Mr. Thespidos that he should give her a little food to have with her in the packing-case.

But she decided that if he had not thought of it, there must be some reason for her to remain hungry.

Mr. Thespidos, having put on his jacket and hat, looked at his watch.

"We must be moving soon," he said. "Drink up your coffee. It will make you feel better."

Corena thought that was good sense.

She quickly drank what was left in the cup and filled it half-full again from the coffee-pot.

She was just stirring in some sugar, when she suddenly felt very strange.

The room seemed to be moving around her.

As she tried to hold on to the desk, her hand groped for it as if it would not obey her.

Then, as she tried to ask what was happening, the words would not come to her lips.

A darkness came up from the floor to cover her.

chapter four

LORD Warburton left his house in extremely high spirits.

He had said good-bye to Charles, who said:

"I only hope, Orion, that either you find your Aphrodite quickly, or you give up the chase and come home. There is a great deal for you to do here, most especially with your horses."

"At the moment I am trying to win a greater prize," Lord Warburton replied.

"I would feel happier if your Aphrodite were flesh and blood, for making you follow her all over the world!"

"In which case I would undoubtedly not return for years!" Lord Warburton replied with irrefutable logic.

Charles laughed.

"I can see you are intent on behaving like a Crusading Knight without actually hearing the cries of the 'Damsel in distress,' or seeing her."

Lord Warburton smiled.

"The trouble with you, Charles," he said, "is that you are romantic, something I gave up years ago and have never regretted it!"

Charles knew this was true, but he merely laughed and teased Lord Warburton until he said:

"I shall find it a relief to be by myself in the yacht and to be able to sit reading Sophocles, who made a great deal more sense than you are making!"

"I am sorry for you," Charles replied, "and all I can remember of Sophocles is that he said:

"'Many marvels there are, but none so marvellous as man.'"

"I suppose that is what you are thinking you are at the moment!"

"If I had something hard near me, I would throw it at you!" Lord Warburton replied. "At the same time, I hope you have noted that Sophocles was praising men, not women!"

"You are hopeless! I wash my hands of you!" Charles exclaimed.

The two men were still joking when after an early breakfast Lord Warburton set off to the same Railway Junction from which Corena had travelled the day before.

There was a first-class carriage reserved for him.

There was another in a second-class coach for his valet and the Courier who always travelled with him to see that everything was perfectly arranged up to the moment of his departure.

He was, as it happened, much looking forward to

being at sea again and engaging in further trials for his yacht.

The *Sea-Serpent,* as he had named it, was fitted with a great number of gadgets which he had invented himself.

Although few people realised it, Lord Warburton had a mind which sprang easily and masterfully from one subject to another, despite the fact that his main interest was Greece.

Because he expected perfection in everything he did, there was nothing that aroused his interest more quickly than the knowledge that some new mechanical device would be an improvement to his yacht.

Similarly, for his farms new and useful vehicles or pieces of machinery were ordered immediately.

If he found a mistake in a book he was reading, he wrote at once to the publishers to point it out.

As he thought of the *Sea-Serpent,* he was quite certain that before he reached Greece he would be able to think of some improvement which would make it even more outstanding.

Actually that would be hard, for every ship-builder and every prospective owner who saw it was amazed at the many innovations it contained which were lacking in the yachts belonging to other people.

"How the devil did you think of anything so useful as the way you have built your galley?" the Duke of Melchester had asked him.

"The old one obviously caused much waste of time and inconvenience for the Chefs compared with what I have designed," Lord Warburton replied.

The Prince of Wales was equally impressed with the comfort of the cabins when Lord Warburton had taken him on a short trip earlier in the year.

"One thing about which there can be no argument, Warburton," he said, "is that you live like a Lord!"

They had both laughed at this.

Lord Warburton, however, knew there was a great deal of truth in what the Prince had said.

He, however, thought with satisfaction that he would have no guests on the *Sea-Serpent* on this voyage to Greece.

He had found it was always a mistake to take a lady aboard unless he could be absolutely certain there would not be the slightest ripple of the waves as the yacht passed through the Bay of Biscay.

As it was impossible to ensure this at any time of the year, he had decided long ago that if he went abroad by sea, he travelled alone, or else with only male companions.

Women were always sea-sick, which inevitably led them to whine and complain.

What was more, if the sea was really rough, they declared they were frightened unless they were in the safety and security of his arms.

In the train Lord Warburton read the newspapers, but he was, nevertheless, thinking only of Greece.

Perhaps this time, by some miracle, he would find the statue of Aphrodite he had heard of but had never been completely convinced of its existence.

Yet his friend, a man who was extremely knowledgeable, but who was growing old, had written to tell him of the rumours.

They were of a statue answering the description of the one he was seeking.

It was believed she was somewhere in Delphi, perhaps near the Temple of Athena Pronaia.

Lord Warburton would never have believed such a

rumour coming from anyone else, but his friend, who was called Koukali, was different.

He never exaggerated and never, as long as he had known him, had he raised hopes unless there was some chance of their being substantiated.

Lord Warburton remembered that Koukali had on several occasions spoken of astrologers and clairvoyants in whom he was interested.

For the first time, it struck him that the information about the Aphrodite might have come from them rather than from a more reliable, or perhaps it would be fairer to say, some more material source.

If this was the case, he had an uncomfortable feeling that he might be setting out on a "wild goose chase."

There had been so much digging recently in Delphi that it was hard to believe that anything had escaped the notice of the French or the English.

But, of course, one never knew.

He remembered finding some years ago at Delos, near the cave sanctuary of Apollo, a small but quite exquisite marble hand of a child.

It was extraordinary that it had been there for all those years, but no one had discovered it before.

He had brought it back to England with him and had it set up on a special plinth in Warburton Park.

Whenever he looked at it he felt that it had waited for him all the centuries that had passed since it had been carved.

It had been meant by some Power which controlled such matters that it should eventually come to him for safe-keeping.

He was well aware that it could have been found by one of the "sharks" who had discovered that selling pieces of Greek statuary was an easy way of making money.

It might then have been sold to someone who might not have properly appreciated it or been able to display it so artistically as at Warburton Park.

"Perhaps something like that is waiting for me now!" he told himself.

He felt an urgency that the voyage should soon be over.

Then he would be able to look, as his friend Koukali had suggested, near the Temple of Athena.

The train arrived in Folkestone late in the afternoon, and a carriage was waiting for Lord Warburton at the station to drive him down to the Quay.

He looked with delight at his yacht, where it lay at anchor, the lines of it.

He thought it looked more like a greyhound than a serpent, and was just as swift.

The Captain was waiting at the head of the gangway to say:

"Welcome aboard, My Lord!"

"I am glad to be back with you," Lord Warburton replied truthfully. "I hope we can start immediately the luggage arrives from the station."

"That is what I anticipated you would want, My Lord," the Captain replied.

Lord Warburton walked into the Saloon.

He noted with pleasure how attractive it looked decorated with the pretty chintz he had chosen to match the green walls.

There was a green carpet on the floor, and the chairs and sofas that were battened down were the most comfortable obtainable.

There was a bookcase filled with books, the majority of them concerned with Greece.

The pictures on the walls had been specially chosen by Lord Warburton and depicted his favourite views painted by Greek artists.

There was, naturally, one of the Temple of Apollo, and beside it was one of the Temple of Athena which Lord Warburton studied now with even greater interest than he had ever done before.

He wondered if he was clairvoyant enough for the spirits of the past to speak to him and tell him where the statue lay hidden beneath the fallen stones.

The three high pillars still standing of the Temple made it one of the most beautiful buildings in Delphi, an architectural masterpiece of the fourth century B.C.

Then he laughed at his fantasy and went along the deck to the bridge to watch the Captain take the ship out of port and into the English Channel.

Because he was so interested and had no wish to go below until it was dark, Lord Warburton dined late.

Despite the fact that he was alone, he had, as usual, without even questioning it, changed for dinner.

Sitting at the top of the table, he enjoyed an excellent meal which was prepared and served with the same perfection he expected and received at the Park.

He drank a little champagne, and after dinner accepted a small glass of brandy from his Chief Steward.

Then, when the servants withdrew, he settled himself comfortably in one of his deep armchairs.

The throbbing of the engines was music in his ears.

He could travel in comfort on an expedition which he found exciting.

He was certain, after what he had said to the Captain,

that the *Sea-Serpent* would break all records in getting him where he wanted to go.

He sat thinking, and when he finally retired to the Master Cabin, it was quite late.

His valet was waiting for him, a man who had served him for over ten years and knew him perhaps better than any other human being did.

"Oi bets you're enjoyin' yerself, M'Lord," Hewlett said with the respectful familiarity of a servant who has special privileges where his master is concerned.

"You know this is what I most enjoy, Hewlett," Lord Warburton replied as he took off his evening-clothes.

"Oi knows it, M'Lord, but you'll never make other people understand what they calls 'a bit o' old stone' means to Yer Lordship!"

"What does it mean to you, Hewlett?" Lord Warburton enquired.

"A chance t' get away from all 'em chattering folk at t'Park, an' women as can't keep their 'ands to themselves!"

It was impossible for Lord Warburton not to laugh.

He was well aware that Hewlett, like himself, was pursued by women, who found him both amusing and attractive.

But they could not, again like his master, entice him up the aisle.

"An' wot might Yer Lordship be alookin' for this time?" Hewlett asked.

Because he was fond of his valet and trusted him more than he trusted anybody else, Lord Warburton told him the truth.

"I am hoping, Hewlett, that I shall find a statue of Aphrodite who, as you know, was the Greek Goddess of Love."

"Sounds interestin', M'Lord," Hewlett said laconi-cally, "but Oi only 'opes she don' go askin' too much o' Yer Lordship!"

Lord Warburton, although he was amused, did not reply, and there was no need, for Hewlett was already leaving his cabin.

"Good-night, M'Lord!" he murmured as he shut the door.

Lord Warburton was smiling as he got into bed.

It pleased him to know that Hewlett enjoyed these expeditions as much as he did.

He was well aware any other servant might find the variations in climate, the effort of digging, and the days and nights of discomfort a burden.

Hewlett, however, took it all in his stride, and invar-iably had something amusing to say which made his master laugh.

The slight rocking of the yacht told him they were out to sea and the "purr" of the engines lulled Lord Warburton to sleep.

*   *   *

Having passed a dreamless night, Lord Warburton awoke to feel full of energy and hurried on deck as soon as he was dressed.

He had been right in thinking that the *Sea-Serpent* could reach fourteen knots.

By the time they were steaming past the coast of northern France and heading South-West across the Bay of Biscay, she was doing over thirteen knots and he was extremely elated.

"If you can keep this up, Captain," he said, "we shall be able to reach Crisa sooner than I expected."

"Is that where you are landing, M'Lord?"

"Yes, but I deliberately have not told anybody so until now."

"I'm glad about that, M'Lord."

The way the Captain spoke made Lord Warburton look at him in surprise.

"Why do you say that?"

"There have been the usual 'Nosey Parkers' asking questions before Your Lordship came on board as to where the yacht was heading."

"The Press?" Lord Warburton enquired.

"I imagine so, M'Lord. They are always inquisitive about members of the aristocracy, and especially Your Lordship."

"Why is that?" Lord Warburton asked sharply.

The Captain thought for a moment. Then he said slowly:

"I suppose, M'Lord, you are more of an enigma than most of the other gentlemen."

"What do you mean?" Lord Warburton enquired, thinking it was a strange word to use.

"Well, M'Lord, you're rich, you're important, you have some of the best horse-flesh in England, but you go off on your own, so to speak, on journeys like the one you're taking now, and nobody knows for certain where they might be able to find you."

Lord Warburton knew this was true.

He had learned a long time ago that it was a great mistake to say where he was going.

He had found in the past there had been friends and acquaintances, and journalists from the newspapers waiting to greet him on his arrival.

It sometimes made it impossible for him to escape the hospitality he had no wish to accept.

It had also often prevented him from setting off immediately on some expedition on which he had set his heart.

This applied particularly when he visited Greece.

Now, he thought with satisfaction, he had been extremely wise in not letting even the Captain be aware of where he was going until the ship had left harbour.

He spent most of the day on the bridge, apart from taking exercise by walking briskly round the deck.

He enjoyed the warmth of the sunshine and the salt on the wind which seemed to sharpen as they neared the Bay of Biscay.

Then the waves began to make it clear that they were in for a rough passage.

* * *

The following morning when Hewlett called Lord Warburton he said:

"If it gets any rougher, M'Lord, Oi thinks it'd be wise to 'ave that crate put in a safer place."

"What crate?" Lord Warburton enquired. "I do not know what you are talking about."

"That large crate marked 'Fragile' which Yer Lordship gave instructions was to be put in th' cabin next door."

Hewlett paused, then said:

"Whoever brought it aboard was stupid enough to set it down in th' middle of th' floor. If it slides about, whatever it contains might get broken."

"I still do not know what you are talking about," Lord Warburton said in a bored voice. "I gave no orders for anything to be brought aboard before I embarked. In fact, nobody knew when I did so, except for the Captain and yourself."

"Well, they tells me as 'ow a crate comes aboard

early on the day we arrived," Hewlett said, "and on Yer Lordship's instructions it were put next t' th' Master Cabin."

Lord Warburton did not speak, and after a moment Hewlett said:

"P'raps Yer Lordship 'ad better look at it when you've 'ad your breakfast."

"I will look at it when I am dressed," Lord Warburton said.

He did not say any more, but he was wondering what the crate contained.

How could anyone early in the morning, before he arrived at six o'clock the same evening, have had any idea that he would be coming aboard?

He had sent a messenger from the Park, calculating that if he went on an earlier train than he took himself, the man should arrive exactly two hours before he did.

That would give the Captain time to get up steam, and the Chefs to take on fresh food.

But not, which was something he disliked, for there to be time for anyone to gossip or speculate as to where he was heading.

It was a routine he had followed now for the last three years and found it suited him.

What was more, there had never been any difficulties with the crew who were always "standing by" at this time of the year, just in case the yacht was needed.

"A crate of—what?" he asked himself as he brushed his hair in front of a mirror.

He was standing with his legs apart to balance himself against the movement of the ship.

Hewlett helped him into his yachting-jacket with its gold buttons.

Then, instead of proceeding up the companionway to

where his breakfast would be waiting for him in the Saloon, he came out of the Master Cabin and opened the door of the cabin next to it.

This was a cabin he had decorated, when he had built the yacht, in a manner appropriate for any woman he might wish to have as his guest.

Its furnishing had been completed before he had decided, after all, that women were a nuisance and his guests would be only men.

The curtains, therefore, which covered the portholes, were a pretty shade of pink with a pattern of lilies on them.

The same material was draped elegantly over the bed from a corola attached to the ceiling.

The bed-spread was of quilted pink stain and the walls were white, so that the whole cabin looked fresh and a perfect background for any woman who might occupy it.

It was, however, at the moment empty except for a large, ugly-looking packing-case which stood in the centre of the floor.

As Hewlett had advisedly said, if the sea grew rougher, it would slide from side to side and damage whatever it contained.

He had been correct in feeling apprehensive, Lord Warburton thought, as he saw a large notice on top of the packing-case on which was printed FRAGILE—THIS SIDE UP—HANDLE WITH CARE.

He looked at it and tried to remember if by any chance he had forgotten that he had ordered extra china, or perhaps glass, for the yacht.

He knew that his secretary, who saw to all these matters, would have replaced immediately on their arrival home from a voyage anything that had been smashed or damaged.

But he could not recall having bought anything himself, and certainly nothing that would require such a large packing-case.

Then he noticed that beside the packing-case there was a trunk, and this, too, seemed strange.

It bore no label, nor were there any initials or, as would have been the case with most of his friends, a coronet emblazoned on it.

As he and Hewlett stood looking at it, a strong wave caused the ship to pitch forward, then back, and they saw the packing-case move slightly.

"You are right, Hewlett," Lord Warburton said. "This should be put in a safer place, although I have not the slightest idea what it contains."

"Shall I open it, M'Lord?"

Hewlett looked at the sides as he spoke, then said in surprise:

"It ain't locked, M'Lord!"

Lord Warburton thought this again was strange, but he merely said:

"Then open it!"

Hewlett pulled at the top, which, surprisingly, did not appear to be fastened down in any way.

Then, as he pulled it off with an ease which he himself thought extraordinary, Lord Warburton stepped forward.

He stiffened and stared with astonishment at what lay inside.

For one moment he thought he must be dreaming and that instead of his going to Greece to seek the Aphrodite Koukali had told him about, Aphrodite had been sent to him.

It took him several seconds, however, before he was aware that what he was seeing was not a marble statue but the head of a woman who was alive and breathing.

She was very pale, which at first had deceived him into thinking she was made of stone, but her eye-lashes were dark against her cheeks.

The hair which was arranged softly against the oval of her forehead was real, and not carved.

Her small, straight nose was that of the Goddess Aphrodite for which Lord Warburton was seeking, and her lips were shaped as he had known they would be, and the small, pointed chin seemed part of his dreams.

Then, as he stared, he heard Hewlett say almost as if he spoke from another world:

"Gor blimey, if it ain't a stowaway!"

His words brought Lord Warburton back to reality.

"A stowaway?" he repeated dazedly.

"That's wot it be, M'Lord, an' unless she's pretend-in' to be asleep, my guess is she's been drugged!"

"I cannot believe it!" Lord Warburton said beneath his breath.

Then, as he bent over the packing-case to make quite sure the woman was actually there, very slowly she opened her eyes.

For a moment she seemed not to focus, then she blinked and opened them again.

As Lord Warburton and Hewlett watched, silent in their astonishment, she drew a deep breath.

In a frightened little voice they could hardly hear, she said:

"W-where . . . am . . . I?"

As she spoke, Lord Warburton was finally convinced that she was human, and his fancy that she was Aphrodite was replaced by an irritation at having been deceived.

At the same time, he saw now that she was covered with a white cloth up to her chin and her head was resting on a white pillow.

It had been easy, therefore, to imagine, with the waves dashing against the port-holes and darkening the cabin, that she was made of marble.

He did not reply, and as her eyes opened wide she was aware of him looking down at her.

It was then she gave an involuntary little cry as if she were afraid and said:

"Oh . . . it is . . . you!"

The words were indistinct, but just clear enough for him to hear them.

"If you know who I am," he remarked, "perhaps you will inform me what you are doing here."

Corena looked away from him to the side of the packing-case.

Then, as if it gradually registered in her mind that he was waiting for an answer, she asked:

"Am I . . . on your . . . yacht?"

"You are!" Lord Warburton confirmed. "And not surprisingly, I would like an explanation as to why you are here!"

Corena made an effort as if to raise herself.

Then as she did so, everything seemed to swim around her and she was conscious that her throat was dry, and so were her lips.

"Could I . . . please . . . have something . . . to drink?" she asked hesitatingly.

As she spoke she thought she must have been drugged, but knew it was something she could not explain to Lord Warburton.

Gradually her mind seemed to be clearing.

She remembered Mr. Thespidos telling her to drink up her coffee, and then having drunk it she could remember nothing more.

She knew now he had rendered her unconscious so that she would make no fuss when she was incarcerated in the crate which had been waiting for her downstairs.

They must have carried her aboard just as he had told her he intended to do.

Now, when they were at sea, Lord Warburton had discovered her.

Because it was all so frightening, as it became clearer in her mind she could feel herself begin to tremble.

She kept her eyes shut until she heard a voice say:

"I've brought some coffee for the young lady, M'Lord. If she's bin drugged, as she must 'ave been, it'll clear 'er mind quicker."

"Drugged?" Lord Warburton said sharply. "What makes you think she has been drugged?"

Hewlett made no answer; he was bending down inside the crate, lifting Corena's head a little and holding the cup containing the coffee to her lips.

She sipped it gratefully.

She was wondering as she did so what she should say to explain her presence, and wondering, too, how long she had been aboard the yacht.

Then as she drank half the cup of coffee Hewlett put her head back on the pillow and said to Lord Warburton:

"I thinks, M'Lord, it'd be a good idea if you'd give the young lady time to come round, so to speak. If you go up and 'ave your breakfast, I'll fetch her somethin' to eat and drink, an' after that she'll be able to talk."

Corena closed her eyes again.

She was praying that Lord Warburton would agree to what the man who she thought must be his valet had suggested.

It would give her time to think.

"Very well, Hewlett," Lord Warburton said after a moment's pause. "I will have my breakfast, as you suggest. Make it clear to the young woman when you have revived her that I wish to speak to her in the Saloon as soon as possible."

"Very good, M'Lord."

Corena heard Lord Warburton walk from the cabin, moving carefully, she thought, against the ship's roll.

Then, as the door closed behind him, Hewlett put his hands on her shoulders and lifted her so that she could sit up.

"Now, you let me help you out of your coffin, Miss!" he said cheerfully. "Then, if you lies down on th' bed, I'll get you somethin' to eat and some more coffee. You'll soon be as right as rain!"

Because it sounded so sensible, Corena forced herself to reply.

"Thank . . . you," she said faintly. "I do feel rather . . . muzzy."

"'Course you do!" Hewlett said. "Now, come along, heave-ho! an' you'll soon be yerself again."

He lifted her out of the packing-case and half-carried her, although she tried to walk, across to the bed.

Because of the movement of the ship, she found herself falling against him.

Then as Hewlett lifted her body onto the bed, she sank back with relief against the pillows.

Only as she did so did she have the terrifying thought that perhaps Mr. Thespidos had undressed her and taken away her clothes.

She opened her eyes tentatively and saw to her relief that she was still wearing the blue gown in which she had travelled to Folkestone.

At least it was decent, but the horror of what Mr. Thespidos had suggested to her in relation to Lord Warburton had already come back into her mind.

She had been afraid that in making her look like a statue and covering her with a white cloth to make it appear that she was made of stone, he had tried to make the impression even more convincing by leaving her naked.

It was such a relief to see that that fear was unfounded, she shut her eyes again.

She wanted to drift away into the unconsciousness that had overtaken her in Mr. Thespidos's office.

She wondered now what he had given her and thought it must have been laudanum or some other drug.

She had no idea for how long she had remained unconscious and thought that was something about which she must enquire of the valet when he returned.

He had already left the cabin, presumably to get her breakfast.

She thought it would be pleasant if she could wash her hands and face.

But it was too much effort, and she did in fact feel very strange and as if she were only half in possession of her senses.

In fact, when after what seemed a long time he spoke to her, she thought his voice came from far away.

It would be easier to ignore it than to answer it.

Then he was giving her more coffee to drink.

As the warmth and strength of it seemed to pass down her throat and into her body she felt that everything had become more real and coherent.

"Now, what I wants you to do, Miss," Hewlett said, "is to 'ave somethin' t'eat, then 'ave a good sleep. We're runnin' into some rough weather, an' you'll be better off in bed than flounderin' about breakin' your arms or legs, if you're not careful!"

Corena thought this was a good idea.

Then she said in a voice that was little more than a whisper:

"Does . . . His Lordship . . . want to . . . see me?"

"'Is Lordship can wait!" Hewlett replied. "Now, just you do as I says, an' while you're eatin' your egg before it gets cold, I'll unpack your trunk!"

He made Corena feel that she was in the hands of a kind and competent Nanny.

Since Nannies always had to be obeyed, it was so much easier to do what he said than to argue.

She ate the egg, drank some more coffee, and realised when she had done so that Hewlett had unpacked most of her trunk.

He had even hung up her gowns in a fitted cupboard.

Then he put one of her nightgowns down on the bed and said:

"Now, make an effort, Miss, and do as I say. You'll find a bathroom on the other side of the cabin, but be careful 'ow you walks."

He picked up the tray and went on:

"I'll be back in quarter-of-an hour, and expect to find you undressed and in bed!"

He did not wait for her to answer, but went from the cabin.

Slowly, because her head felt as if it were filled with cotton-wool, Corena climbed out of the bed and, moving very cautiously, reached the bathroom.

Vaguely she was aware that it was very unusual to

have a private bathroom attached to a cabin in any yacht afloat.

However, it was difficult to think of anything except herself.

She pulled off her clothes one by one, and washed in the basin, feeling it was too much trouble to run the bath.

She put on her nightgown and crept, again afraid of being tossed from side to side, back to bed.

It seemed like a haven of security as she reached it.

As she slipped between the sheets and lay back against the pillows, she was aware that her head was aching and she wanted more than anything else to sleep.

She did not hear Hewlett come back into the cabin and look at her with satisfaction.

Nor did she hear him tidying her clothes away from the bathroom or pull the curtains over the port-holes.

She would, however, have been amused if she could have heard the conversation he had later with Lord Warburton.

"What is that young woman doing now?" Lord Warburton asked as soon as Hewlett went into the Saloon.

"Sleepin', M'Lord, like a new-born baby! An' that's what she's likely to be doin' for the next twenty-four hours!"

"What the devil is she doing aboard?" Lord Warburton enquired. "Who brought her here?"

"I've made enquiries, M'Lord, as I was certain you'd ask that question," Hewlett replied. "There seems to 'ave been two men as brought her aboard. It was a steward as sees them and spoke to them, an' who showed them down below. 'E says as 'ow they was foreigners."

Lord Warburton stared at him.

"Did he say what nationality?"

"'E didn't know, M'Lord, but the Chef as was listenin' says 'ow he is certain they was Greek."

Lord Warburton sat up in his chair.

"Greek?" he ejaculated.

"Seems strange, M'Lord, they should be Greek, when that's jus' where we're goin'!"

"Very strange!" Lord Warburton agreed. "I wonder if she is Greek too?"

He was speaking his thoughts aloud, but Hewlett answered him.

"She speaks English all right, M'Lord," he said, "but she's a woman, an' there ain't a woman born as doesn't know every trick in the calendar! So she may be Greek, or she may be a 'ottentot for all I knows!"

Lord Warburton made no reply.

He was frowning and Hewlett was aware that he was irritated.

Knowing his master's moods better than anybody else, he decided this was the moment to retreat.

chapter five

CORENA awoke and found to her relief that she felt her normal self.

For the first time, she was able to look around the cabin and thought it was very pretty.

She liked the pink curtains with their white lilies.

She realised, although she had never been in such a large yacht before, that all the fittings were very cleverly designed and attached to the walls.

There was a large mirror with a lot of drawers under it, which made it an excellent dressing-table.

The cupboards were concealed by being white like the rest of the cabin.

The bed, too, was very comfortable, and she lay for a little while seeing the sunshine flooding in every time the ship rolled.

She fancied, although she was not sure, that the sea was smoother than it had been when she went to sleep.

Yet it was difficult to remember anything except that her head had not seemed to belong to her.

Suddenly she remembered, now that she was herself again, she would have to face Lord Warburton.

She felt a little tremor of fear run through her.

As she did so, there was a discreet knock, and before she could answer, Hewlett put his head round the door.

"'Mornin', Miss!" he said. "I thought you'd be awake, and I needn't ask if you've 'ad a good night. I knows you 'ave!"

"I slept . . . peacefully," Corena replied, "and I remember now that you unpacked for me and gave me something . . . to eat. Thank you . . . very much!"

"That's all right, Miss," Hewlett said, "an' I expect now you'd like me to run your bath, then when you're dressed, you'll be able to go up to the Saloon and talk to 'Is Lordship."

He did not wait for Corena's reply, but disappeared into the bathroom.

She wondered if she could say she was too ill and would like to stay in bed for at least a few more hours before she encountered Lord Warburton.

Then she knew she was being cowardly.

When Hewlett told her he had run her bath and not to let it get cold, she knew she must get up.

"I'll be back in quarter-of-an-hour to button your gown," he said, "and it's somethin' I'm real good at!"

He gave her an impish grin and went from the cabin.

Corena realised she still had to walk carefully in case she staggered, and to hold on to something when the yacht rolled in a deep trough.

She managed to have a bath and enjoy it.

She found that Hewlett had laid out all her underclothes on a chair.

She did not feel embarrassed because he was a man.

Yesterday he had seemed so like an experienced and kindly Nanny that she still thought of him that way.

She had buttoned the top buttons at the back of her gown and was doing her hair when he came back.

"That's better!" he approved. "You'll feel your old self, Miss, soon as you've been out in th' fresh air. But you'll need a shawl; it's still a bit nippy outside."

He buttoned up her gown, brought a warm shawl from where he had placed it in the wardrobe, and said as if he were speaking to a shy child:

"Come along now, the first step's always th' hardest!"

Corena gave a little laugh.

At the same time, she had the feeling that Hewlett was well aware that the first step as far as she was concerned was to encounter his Master.

He helped her up the companionway.

Then, as she longed to go through the glass door which led onto the deck, he opened the one which led into the Saloon.

"'Ere's the young lady, M'Lord," he announced in a cheerful voice, "and feelin' quite 'erself."

Corena thought that was an over-statement.

She looked across the Saloon at Lord Warburton, who was seated in one of the comfortable chairs with a book in his hand.

She felt frightened and was wondering frantically what she should say as she walked a little unsteadily towards him.

Before she reached him he half-rose in his chair and indicated one opposite him, saying:

"I should sit down as quickly as possible. There is

still a considerable swell, but we have passed through the worst of it."

Corena obeyed him.

As she was facing the sunshine coming through the glass windows behind Lord Warburton's head, he could see her very clearly.

As her eyes were dazzled by the sun, it was more difficult to see him.

She sat back in her chair, as if she felt it protected her.

Then, as she looked at Lord Warburton with her eyes wide and frightened, he thought once again that she looked like a Greek goddess rather than an English girl.

It was an effort, although he would not admit it to himself, to ask:

"Perhaps you would explain to me why you are here."

It was a question that Corena had been expecting.

Yet, when it came, everything seemed to fly out of her head and she could only stare at him, thinking he was very handsome, but extremely formidable.

She tried in vain to formulate what would seem a sensible answer to his question, and after what seemed a long pause he said:

"I am waiting! There must be some reason for you to be aboard my yacht."

She thought for the first time that he had obviously not recognised her from her last visit at Warburton Park.

It was not really surprising, considering she had called on him wearing a black bonnet and veil which partially obscured her face, besides the tinted spectacles which belonged to her father.

Just for a moment it flashed through her mind that

perhaps the best thing to say was that she had no idea why she had been brought here.

Then, fearing that he might in that case put her off at Gibraltar, she said hesitatingly:

"I—it was the only . . . way I could . . . reach my . . . father."

Lord Warburton stared at her. Then he said:

"Are you telling me you are Miss Melville?"

"Y-yes."

"So you were determined to travel with me rather than by train!"

"I . . . I thought it would be . . . quicker," Corena said faintly.

Now she was tense, waiting for him to rage at her, and when he did speak without raising his voice, it was a relief.

"It seems extraordinary," he said, "for you to be so persistent, and I cannot imagine that the difference in time of the journey was your only reason for foisting yourself on me."

Corena drew in her breath, thinking that he had given her an idea for an explanation that would sound logical.

"I thought, My Lord," she said, "that as . . . you are so important . . . and have a great deal of influence . . . you might . . . help . . . my father when I reach him."

Again Lord Warburton stared at her.

"Surely Sir Priam, even if he is ill, is not alone, but has servants or friends to attend to him?"

"I . . . I am not . . . certain of that," Corena said. "When Papa is exploring a site where he thinks he might . . . find something . . . important or excavating, he must be . . . alone."

"Are you telling me that your father is an Archaeologist?" Lord Warburton asked.

"Yes, My Lord. He is obsessed with anything Greek and is happy only when he is looking for forgotten sculptures which he can bring home with him."

"I had no idea of that," Lord Warburton said, "and who was it you had said, that informed you that your father is ill?"

Corena had to think quickly, then after a little hesitation she said:

"A Greek who had ... travelled to London from ... Crisa brought me a ... message from ... my father."

Because it was a lie, she could not look at Lord Warburton as she spoke.

She had the feeling, however, that he was scrutinising her closely, as if he suspected she might be deceiving him.

"Surely, if you wished to go to your father," he said after a moment, "there would be some relation who could travel with you, or at least you could have been chaperoned by an older woman?"

"There was ... nobody."

"I find that hard to believe," Lord Warburton said, "and you are certainly breaking all the conventions, Miss Melville, not only by coming aboard my yacht in such an extraordinary manner, but also by journeying with me alone."

"I will ... not be a ... nuisance ... I promise you ... My Lord," Corena said quickly. "In fact, you need not even ... see me ... if you do not ... wish to."

She was sure he was looking sceptical, and she went on quickly:

"I will stay in my own cabin and go out on deck only when you are ... busy or ... asleep."

Her words seemed to tumble over themselves.

Before Lord Warburton could speak, she knew that

he was considering whether it would be best to send her overland at the next convenient port of call.

"Please . . ." she begged. "Please let me . . . stay with you. I would be . . . afraid to travel . . . alone."

She looked so young and at the same time so agitated as she spoke that Lord Warburton thought that was not surprising.

However, he disliked being forced into doing what he had already refused to do, and he thought the girl opposite him was not only unpredictable, but over-persistent.

At the same time, she was very young.

While she was speaking he could not get it out of his head that she might have been one of the goddesses from Olympus asking for his protection.

Aloud, he replied:

"I will think over what you have suggested, Miss Melville, though I cannot help feeling it is very impractical."

"But . . . I may stay . . . on board?" Corena asked.

For the first time since they had been talking there was just a faint twist at the corner of Lord Warburton's lips as he replied:

"I can hardly ask you to leave immediately. It is a long way to swim to the coast of Portugal unless you can produce a dolphin to carry you!"

"I only wish I . . . could have a . . . dolphin!" Corena said in a low voice, "like the one that guided Apollo to Crisa . . . where I . . . want you to . . . take me."

"If your father is an Archaeologist, I presume you know a great deal about Greece," Lord Warburton remarked somewhat grudgingly.

Corena smiled.

"My great-grandmother, My Lord, was Greek, and

my grandmother, who was very beautiful, resembled her."

"I presume that is the reason why your father finds that country so interesting."

"He loves every stick and stone of it," Corena answered, "and it is because he was so unhappy after . . . Mama died that I was . . . glad he was . . . going back there."

As she spoke, she thought of what had happened to him since and how he was a prisoner of the bestial Mr. Thespidos.

She was not aware that her eyes were very expressive, and Lord Warburton said:

"I should not be too anxious about him. He may be suffering only from one of the fevers which are so prevalent in that part of the world, and by the time you arrive, he should be perfectly well."

"I am . . . praying . . . so," Corena murmured.

Then because Lord Warburton had spoken in a kinder way than he had before, she said:

"You will . . . take me to . . . Crisa?"

There was a distinct pause before Lord Warburton replied:

"You make it very difficult for me to refuse, considering there is nobody to accompany you, and you are far too—young—to travel alone."

He had nearly said "lovely," then bit back the word at the last moment.

Corena's eyes widened.

"You will . . . take me? Oh . . . thank you . . . thank you! How can I . . . tell you how . . . grateful I am?"

"I assure you it is against both my instinct and my wish to travel alone," Lord Warburton said as if he felt he must assert himself.

"I promise you I will be as little trouble as possible," Corena said humbly. "Shall I go . . . away now?"

"I think it might be a mistake," Lord Warburton replied, "when you have been unconscious for so long, to move about too soon, and also the ship is till rolling."

Corena waited, her eyes on his face, until he added a little reluctantly:

"You can stay here. I shall be going out myself in a little while to take some exercise."

"Thank you . . . thank you . . . very much."

There was silence until Lord Warburton remarked:

"I have the idea that you might like to look at my book-shelves."

Corena answered simply:

"I would love to, but I was too nervous to ask you if I might."

"They are at your disposal."

She flashed him a radiant smile, then rose and, moving slowly in order to keep her balance, she reached the book-case and knelt down in front of it.

She was aware as she did so that Lord Warburton was watching her.

When she saw the books, she knew there were some "old friends" and others she had been wanting to read for a long time.

She saw a book of the plays of Sophocles which contained his play *Ajax*.

She opened it and was at once so immersed in reading one of her favourite passages that she started as Lord Warburton spoke.

She found he had moved without her being aware of it, and was just behind her.

"What do you find so interesting?" he enquired.

As if he had been her father asking the question, she replied:

"I was reading what I think is appropriate to what is happening to us:

'Let the Dawn ride in
On silver horses lighting up the sky
The winds abate and leave the groaning sea
To sleep awhile.'

Her voice was very musical as she translated the words into English.

She was, in fact, almost reciting from memory rather than following the lines with her eyes.

There was a little silence. Then Lord Warburton asked incredulously:

"Are you telling me that you can read the book you are holding in your hand?"

"I have read it before, My Lord, with my father."

"It seems extraordinary, Miss Melville! I have never met a young woman who is interested in Sophocles, let alone able to read what he had written!"

"I have told you that I have Greek blood in my veins," Corena replied, "so perhaps it is easier for me than for somebody who is wholly English."

Lord Warburton sat down in a chair just beside her, then he said:

"Because you have Greek blood in you, which I have, too, do you think that is the reason why we are drawn to Greece, and why it interests us more than any other country in Europe?"

He was assuming that Corena felt the same way he did, but it did not seem strange.

"What interests us," she replied, "is not the Greece of to-day or the people who now call themselves Greek."

She thought of Mr. Thespidos as she spoke, and shivered before she said:

"The Greeks we are talking about are those who brought something new to the world when it was least expecting it."

Lord Warburton did not speak, but she knew he was listening as she continued:

"It was Greek philosophy that influenced the Greek-speaking fathers of the Church and gave us Christianity as we know it."

Still Lord Warburton did not speak, and she went on:

"I am told that all the images of Buddha in the Far East can be traced back to portraits of Alexander, who was believed in the Eastern Provinces to be Apollo incarnate."

She made an expressive gesture with her hands as she said:

"Think what we owe to the Greeks at the beginning of civilisation as we know it, the beginning of rational thought."

She thought Lord Warburton made a little sound of agreement, but actually it was one of surprise before she finished:

"Papa always said they built the most beautiful Temples in carved marble with a delicacy of strength that has never been surpassed!"

Her voice was almost rapturous as she added:

"But what is more important is that they set in motion the questing mind which refused to believe there are any bounds to reason."

As Corena said the last words, it was as if she were sounding a trumpet-call.

Then, as she looked at Lord Warburton, she realised he was staring at her as if in sheer astonishment.

Quite suddenly she felt shy and a little abashed, as if she had shown off in front of him, and it had been the wrong thing to do.

Then to her surprise he bent forward in his chair to ask harshly:

"Who taught you all that? Who told you to say it to me?"

Her eyes widened and seemed to fill her whole face.

"I . . . I do not know . . . what you . . . mean."

"I think you do!" Lord Warburton said. "You have been told that I am interested in Greece and somebody has instructed you how to speak of it."

"That is not . . . true."

She put back the book of Sophocles on the shelf and said:

"I must apologise for boring Your Lordship. It would be best if I returned to my cabin."

She would have risen to her feet, but Lord Warburton put out his hand to prevent her from doing so.

"Stay where you are," he said. "I want to know more about you and to make up my mind if you are genuine or simply play-acting."

Because it sounded so ridiculous, Corena laughed.

"I promise Your Lordship that while I spoke without thinking, it is the way my father and I talk together when he is at home. I forgot for the moment that I was with a stranger who . . . might not . . . understand."

"I *do* understand," Lord Warburton contradicted. "At the same time, it surprises me that you should speak like that—unless you have been very well rehearsed."

103

He seemed to add the last words as an after-thought.

It flashed through Corena's mind that he was deliberately trying to be sceptical and suspected her of intriguing to deceive him.

To a certain extent that was true, but not in the way which he suspected.

His books, if nothing else, told her how knowledgeable he was.

How interesting she thought it would be if she could talk to him naturally, without there being a barrier between them.

It was a barrier erected by his resentment of her having been smuggled aboard and her fear of what Mr. Thespidos would do when they arrived at Crisa.

For a moment she put that away from her mind, and trying to speak lightly, she said:

"If Your Lordship would ever condescend to visit our house, which is in a way a faint echo of yours, I think you would be surprised."

"Why?" Lord Warburton enquired.

"Because you would see the antiques which my father has collected over the years, and would find a great many book-shelves filled, as yours are, with the history of the Greeks."

"I hope when I return to England," Lord Warburton replied, "that I may have the pleasure of calling on you."

"And I hope Papa and I might see your treasures!" Corena said impulsively.

As she spoke, an icy hand seemed to clutch at her heart as she remembered that if her father came home, Lord Warburton would have to stay behind.

Once again Mr. Thespidos was menacing her like a great black evil bird of prey.

She looked at Lord Warburton, seeing him not as a handsome man sitting back comfortably in an armchair, but being tortured by Mr. Thespidos.

He and his confederates, being both avaricious and unscrupulous, would try to extract information from him by any means.

The idea was horrifying, but she told herself she must think of nothing except saving her father.

He was in Mr. Thespidos's power, and the only way she could save him was to do as that evil man had told her to do and exchange one prisoner for another.

For a moment she wanted to scream because it was so horrifying.

Then she heard Lord Warburton saying in a very different tone of voice:

"Who has upset you? Why are you so frightened?"

She wanted to tell him the truth, but Mr. Thespidos had warned her that if she did so, she would sign her father's death warrant.

"I . . . I am just . . . afraid," she said quickly, "that by the time we arrive in Greece Papa will be worse . . . and I will not be able to . . . look after him."

What she said sounded reasonable, but Lord Warburton's acute perception told him there was something wrong, and what she said did not ring true.

To test her, he quoted in Greek some words from Sophocles's play *Ajax* which she had just replaced in the book-case:

> "Great Sun,
> Pull up your golden-harnessed horses
> Over my native land, and tell this story
> Of death and ruin to my aged father . . ."

He thought as he spoke that if Corena were play-acting as he suspected, and been taught certain lines to impress him, then it was unlikely she would know the whole passage or understand what he had just said.

As he finished, he realised she was looking at him with an expression of fear that could not have been assumed.

"Why did you say . . . that? Why did you . . . quote those . . . lines?" she asked a little incoherently. "Do you feel . . . instinctively that . . . Papa is d-dead?"

The way she spoke was so agitated that Lord Warburton put out his hand to re-assure her.

"No, of course not," he said. "I was just testing you to see if you understood what I was saying."

"But . . . why did you choose those particular lines . . . why did they . . . come to your mind?" she asked.

Then, as if she were afraid to say any more, she rose to her feet and moved away from him.

She opened one of the windows that looked onto the deck.

She stood staring out at the sea, with its white-topped waves, but she could see only her father's face, feeling that he was calling to her, needing her help.

Lord Warburton watched her.

He thought that the sun on her hair and her clear-cut profile as she raised her eyes to the sky were lovelier than anything he had ever seen or imagined he might find.

Yet his cold, logical mind told him there was something wrong.

There was something incongruous in her story apart from the fact of her having stowed away on board and being so proficient in the language that meant so much to him.

106

It flashed through his mind that perhaps she was not real.

She was a superhuman being who, like the gods themselves, had come down from the heights to bewilder poor mortals.

Then he could hear Charles laughing at him and teasing him for being imaginative.

He would say with a twinkle in his eye that of course Miss Melville was a perfectly ordinary young woman.

It was just that she had had a classical education and there was an obvious explanation, he would suggest, for her presence.

It was doubtful, Lord Warburton reflected, that she had thought out these dramatics by herself.

Whoever had brought her aboard certainly had a hand in it.

He had not forgotten that his Chef had thought the men to be Greek.

They at least would have appreciated her looks and the fact that she resembled, however much he tried to doubt it, the statues of Aphrodite, statues that were to be found not only in the museums of the world, but in his own house.

The whole story was just too clever to be true.

Her father ill in Greece, the beautiful girl who resembled a goddess and who spoke Ancient Greek smuggled aboard the yacht of the one man in a million who would really appreciate her.

It flashed through Lord Warburton's mind that they were travelling together without a chaperone.

Perhaps Sir Priam would appear at the end of the voyage and would not be ill, not in need of his daughter's care and attention.

Instead, he would be an irate father demanding at the

point of a loaded pistol that having ruined her reputation he must now make reparation by marrying her.

This was certainly a possibility, and yet when he looked at Corena, it was impossible to think that she would be a party to such a plot.

At the same time, she was genuinely afraid.

Yet, being so very observant, he thought that it was not a fear that a young girl would feel because her father might be dying.

It was something deeper, more fundamental, more threatening to her personally.

These ideas racing through his mind stimulated him, and he felt excited by the problem in the same way as when there was a statue waiting for him to discover it.

Just as Lord Warburton's interest was aroused by a new gadget for his yacht, this puzzle was making his mind work like a well-oiled machine.

He was determined to discover the truth about Miss Melville, and he thought it might not be very difficult.

Few women, he thought without conceit, found it easy to resist him.

In fact the "boot was usually on the other foot," and he more often resisted them than they him.

All he had to do was to apply new tactics to the problem and unravel the truth as if it were an ancient relic many feet down beneath the surface.

Corena stood at the window, looking out at the horizon, hoping perhaps she would find beyond it what she was seeking.

Lord Warburton went to her side.

"Suppose we start again?" he said in his most beguiling voice. "First of all, Miss Melville, I think you should tell me your Christian name."

"It is Corena."

"Greek!" Lord Warburton exclaimed. "A 'maiden,' which, of course, is what you are."

She looked at him for a moment, then turned her face away again and wondered why he was interested.

"My name is Orion," he said, "which I feel needs no explanation."

"No, of course not, but I expect, like Papa, you found it a difficult name at School."

Lord Warburton laughed.

"That would certainly have been true had I not been prosaic enough to use my other name, which is George."

Corena laughed.

"That certainly does not suit you as a student of Ancient Greece."

"Now we are introduced properly," Lord Warburton said, "and we can talk of the Greece we love without feeling embarrassed or questioning our reason for it."

"*You* were . . . questioning it—not me!"

"That is true," he agreed, "but you must admit the situation we are both in is rather strange."

"Not if you read the . . . stories of the . . . ancient gods!"

He laughed.

"Of course you are right, Corena, and the gods have special privileges, which makes me feel I can call you by your real name."

It flashed through Corena's mind that they were in a way like two Greek gods journeying homeward after a visit to a place where no one had understood them.

Because she thought he would appreciate what she was thinking, she quoted from Pindar, who had written so many Odes celebrating victories in the Greek Games.

> *"Where are things of the day?*
> *What are we? What are we but*
> *The shadow of a dream?"*

She spoke as if she challenged Lord Warburton, and with hardly a pause he replied with the next line of the poem:

> *"We are all shadows,*
> *But when the shining comes from the hands*
> *of the God*
> *Then the heavenly light falls on men,*
> *And life is all sweetness . . ."*

As he spoke the beautiful words in his deep voice, the sun seemed to illuminate them both with the light that came from Greece.

Corena turned to look at him.

As their eyes met, she felt as if they were speaking in the "honeyed tongues" of Olympus.

There were no more problems or difficulties, for together they were above them all.

She had the strange feeling that Lord Warburton was thinking exactly the same thing.

There was no reason to be afraid, because they were one person, and there was nothing to divide them.

Then as the ship rolled a little more deeply, she put out her hand to hold on to the window ledge and came back to reality.

She was not a goddess linked to a god called Orion, but a girl caught up in a wicked plot to capture as a prisoner a very rich man in exchange for her father's life.

Once again she was aware of Mr. Thespidos hovering menacingly in the background, so that it was difficult for her to think of anything but his evilness, and her father helpless in his hands.

Then, as she felt despairingly that she was alone, there was no one to help her, and that she, too, was a prisoner of Mr. Thespidos, she heard Lord Warburton say:

"Tell me what is troubling you, and trust me. I swear you will not regret it."

*   *   *

When Corena went down to change for dinner, she felt almost ashamed that the day had been so happy.

Except for a few frightening moments when the truth forced itself upon her consciousness, she felt as if she were in a golden dream.

She was well aware that Lord Warburton had set out to assuage her fears.

He wanted to make her feel that she could trust him with the secret of what was upsetting her and that he could solve all her problems.

Because it was easier to swim with the tide than against it, she had allowed herself to be beguiled into talking with him as she might have talked with her father.

They spoke of the gods and goddesses who she often thought were more real and familiar to her than young people of her own generation.

The light of Greece which was a divine radiance illuminated not only what they saw, but what they felt.

Because Lord Warburton was so intelligent and, above all, so well read, he made Corena feel as if she were a flower opening to the warmth of the sun.

They talked, argued, and capped each other's quotations.

Without either of them being aware of it, the yacht had moved into a far smoother sea and was no longer rolling.

"How can you know so much at your age?" Lord Warburton asked once. "I have a feeling you have not only studied the Ancient Greeks, but acquired your knowledge in other lives."

"Of course!" Corena agreed. "And I have often wondered whether, if ever I visit Greece, I will recognise where I lived."

"Then I will certainly take you to Mount Olympus!"

"Which . . . from all Papa says . . . is somewhat disappointing."

"It depends on what you expect!" Lord Warburton replied.

"Perhaps it would be a . . . mistake to go there and find that the . . . gods had all . . . departed."

"That is what people think when they are looking only with their eyes."

For a while they sat in silence before Corena said:

"I would love to go to Olympus . . . but perhaps it would be a . . . mistake to risk being . . . disillusioned."

"That is what I am afraid of too," Lord Warburton admitted.

But she knew he was not speaking of Olympus, and his eyes were on her face.

*   *   *

Hewlett had drawn her bath, and when Corena had dried herself, she walked to the wardrobe in her cabin to see what she should wear.

It was then insidiously once again she could hear Mr. Thespidos's oily voice telling her to pack her prettiest dresses.

She felt herself shudder and deliberately reached for the most simple of her evening-gowns.

Because it was white and had little ornamentation except for the softness of some chiffon draped round the neck and over the tops of her arms, she felt she was defying him.

She was not to know that because her gown was so simple, it resembled more than her other dresses the draperies worn by the goddesses.

It was as they had been carved by endless sculptors down the centuries.

She had brought with her no jewellery because her father had always said it was dangerous to travel abroad with jewels.

There was nothing, therefore, to break the exquisite curved line of her neck or spoil the translucency and whiteness of her breasts.

She had no idea as she entered the Saloon where Lord Warburton was waiting for her, that he drew in his breath.

He thought it would be impossible for anyone to look more lovely or more ethereal and, although he hated to admit it, not human.

Corena was, in fact, thinking how magnificent he looked in his evening-clothes.

As he put a glass of champagne into her hand he said:

"I thought we should both drink to-night to the glory of Greece and that somehow, in some way, we can contribute to it."

"That is a wonderful toast," Corena exclaimed. "Perhaps something . . . special will be . . . revealed to us."

"'Make the sky clear, and grant us to see with our eyes. In the light be it,'" Lord Warburton quoted.

She laughed and raised her glass.

Then, as the steward brought in dinner, Corena was aware that for the first time in her life she would be having dinner alone with a man other than her father.

Somewhere at the back of her mind she remembered she had always thought that would be very exciting.

Course succeeded course, each more delicious than the last, and the candles on the table were lit as darkness fell.

She felt sure she had stepped into a dream and that no god could be more handsome, more alluring, or more interesting than Lord Warburton.

They talked on after the servants had removed the table from the centre of the Saloon.

Then, because it was so much warmer than it had been and they were both aware the wind had dropped, they walked out on deck.

Now, when Corena looked up, the stars had come out in the sky and there was a young crescent moon climbing up towards them.

It was so lovely that she threw back her head, unaware it was the time-honoured gesture of a woman who surrenders herself to the gods.

Then she knew that Lord Warburton was very near her and she heard him say very softly:

"How can this have happened? How can you have come to me so unexpectedly? And yet I feel I have known you all through eternity!"

Corena turned her head to look at him and she asked in a soft, hesitating little voice that did not sound like her own:

"Why did you . . . say that? It is . . . what I feel—"

She stopped, thinking what she had been about to say would seem forward and too revealing.

"What you feel too!" Lord Warburton finished. "My dear, what is happening to us was meant to be, and perhaps has been ordained since the very beginning of time."

"Y-you really . . . believe . . . that?"

She whispered because it was impossible to speak any louder.

"I believe it," he said, "and it is only because I am afraid of frightening you that I do not take you in my arms."

He did not touch her, but she felt as if they drew nearer to each other and his lips were not far from hers.

Then as she knew, and it seemed incredible, that it would be right that he should kiss her and she should give him her heart, she remembered Mr. Thespidos!

The thought of him brought Corena back to earth.

With a little cry of horror she put up her hands as if to ward off Lord Warburton.

Without a word, without explanation, she ran away from him.

Moving as swiftly as if all the devils of hell were behind her, she ran towards the sanctuary of her own cabin.

chapter six

LORD Warburton was in love.

He fought against it, denied it, and told himself he was a fool, until finally he capitulated.

What he felt about Corena was different from anything he had ever felt in his life before.

At first he was quite determined he was just fascinated by her lovely face, and, because he was still suspicious, tried to catch her out in a dozen different ways.

Her knowledge of the Greek historians was fantastic, he admitted honestly to himself.

Then as they steamed on, the *Sea-Serpent* breaking the record as he had intended, he knew that he went to sleep at night thinking about Corena and woke up in the morning still thinking of her.

He found her a delight, and what he felt for her he had never felt for any other woman.

The sophisticated Beauties with whom he had had

brief and usually fiery *affaires de coeur* had meant nothing to him—a physical satisfaction, but no more than that.

Other women whom he had met abroad—and it was inevitable that in Paris he took a mistress amongst the *demi-mondaines*—made little impression on him.

Now he could not remember their names, or even what they looked like.

Every day it seemed as if Corena's Grecian beauty imprinted itself not only on his brain but also on his heart.

He had thought it would be easy to attract her into telling him what he wanted to know.

Instead, he found he was up against a barrier he did not understand, and yet was pulsatingly aware was there.

Corena listened to him with her strange sun-flecked green eyes, and at times he was almost sure he saw in them the expression he was seeking.

He was too experienced not to realise when a woman was attracted by him, and he felt certain Corena loved him, and yet he could not be completely sure.

After the first night when she had run away from him, he had been very careful not to frighten her again.

He talked to her of love, which was easy when they spoke of the Greek gods and goddesses.

Yet somehow it never became personal enough for him to put his arms around her and kiss her, as he longed to do.

Although he did not realise it, for the first time in his life Lord Warburton was being forced to pursue a woman rather than have her fall into his arms even before he knew her name.

It was also the first time that he considered her feelings more than his own.

Because Corena was so ethereal, so very vulnerable, he was afraid of upsetting her and seeing an expression of dislike on her face rather than the one for which he longed.

He was aware she was frightened, but of whom or what he could not determine.

He was quite sure it was not himself.

When they were talking Greek together, her eyes would sparkle with the excitement of it.

And there was nothing sinister or restrained about her laughter, which was like the song of the birds.

"I love her!" he told himself as they sailed past Gibraltar into the Mediterranean.

By the time they had reached Sicily he knew he would give everything he possessed to hold Corena in his arms and know that she was his.

Because he was so closely attuned to her, he was aware that as they drew nearer and nearer to Greece, something was perturbing her that she was trying to keep hidden from him.

He would see a stricken look in her eyes which gave him a physical pain because it was so poignant.

Yet he was intelligent enough to realise that if he tried to press her into confiding in him, he might easily frighten her away.

He wanted her to trust him; he wanted her to realise that he would protect her against anything, however terrible it might be.

The days were sunny, and an awning had been erected over the deck.

They would sit in the shade of it in two wicker chairs

with footrests attached and talk animatedly and excitedly about Greece.

It was only at night in his cabin when he thought over what had been said that Lord Warburton was aware Corena blinded him by her beauty.

She also stimulated and inspired him with her mind.

He knew it was not only because she was so knowledgeable and well read.

It was also because she was so genuinely wrapt up in what they were discussing.

It meant as much to her as it would to another woman if he were making love to her.

In fact, that in a way was what he was doing.

He was trying to attract her with his mind.

He found himself in consequence thinking in a way that he was sure the Greeks themselves had thought in ancient times.

Although he knew his mind was linked with Corena's he wanted a great deal more, but was not certain how to obtain it.

A thousand times he was on the brink of telling her of his love.

He wanted to take her in his arms and kiss her lips, which could have been designed by their Creator only for kisses.

But there was something about Corena which prevented him from doing so.

There was an aura about her both of purity and of spirituality, which he thought must have enveloped the young priestess who became the *Pythia* of the Oracle in Delphi.

In the darkness of his cabin Lord Warburton could see Corena taking her place on the trypod.

She would have bathed in the waters of Castalia and drunk from the holy spring.

She would have been assisted into the special robes of prophecy and led into the Temple of Apollo.

She would have passed through the main halls of worship until she reached the *Adyton*.

This was the most sacred part of all, the living place of the god where only the priests were allowed to enter.

He could see it all happening in front of his eyes, and he thought perhaps he himself had been a priest in Delphi.

That was why when he saw Corena, he had known that thousands of years ago he had watched her.

He had seen her fall into a trance and known that the god was present in her.

The first time he had thought of this at night and seen it happening it was a memory that until now had been hidden at the back of his mind.

He had talked to Corena about it the next day.

She had listened intently, then she had said almost as though she spoke to herself:

"Music was played . . . incense was burned . . . and *Pythia* carried a branch of the Holy laurel leaves which were . . . sacred to . . . Apollo in her . . . hand."

She spoke almost beneath her breath, then as Lord Warburton said:

"How do you know that? I do not remember reading it in any book!"

"I must have . . . read it . . . somewhere," Corena said vaguely, "and they also placed in her hands one of the sacred ribbons which bound her to the *omphalos*."

Her voice deepened as she went on:

"They believed it to be the centre of the Universe and the source of all creative power."

Lord Warburton just stared at her.

He realised her eyes were not seeing him or the Saloon in which they were talking.

She was looking back into the past and remembering how the priests were waiting for her to give them the message of Apollo.

It was all so unbelievably strange.

Yet at other times she would laugh with the spontaneous, happy laughter of a child at the stories with which he regaled her concerning the behaviour of the gods.

They played tricks, for instance, on the simple men and women who worshipped them.

Lord Warburton loved her laughter, and he tried to remember stories that were amusing and tales that he had not thought of for years.

Yet he knew as they steamed on and on that what he really wanted to talk to her about was love.

He felt it growing day by day within him, yet he dared not express it in case she fled from him, as Daphne had from Apollo.

"What can I do?" he asked himself every night when they went to their separate cabins. "How can I make her confide in me and tell me what is troubling her?"

He was absolutely convinced that it was not only her fear for her father's health which at times made her seem withdrawn so that he could not reach her.

He supposed he would find out the truth by the time they reached Crisa.

At the same time, he was desperately afraid that once they were there, she would leave him to go to her father's side, and he might never see her again.

The idea made him clench his fists.

He was aware for the first time in his life that love was not the sweet, warm, sentimental thing he had in the past always believed it to be.

It could also be agonising, and make him feel as if a dagger were being thrust into his heart.

He tried to use what he had been told often enough was his charm to make Corena speak.

He could not understand why, just when he thought he was going to be successful, he would see an expression of pain in her eyes.

Then she would turn her head away as if she dared not look at him.

At times, when their eyes met accidentally, they would both be spell-bound.

Everything they had been about to say would fly out of their minds and they were conscious only of each other.

Again with an effort Corena would look away from him and begin to talk of something quite different and the moment would pass.

This would leave him bitterly conscious that he had failed, although why, and what she was hiding, he could not determine.

All he knew was that he loved her and time was passing not slowly, as he had thought it would, but far too quickly.

He was afraid that when they reached Greece he would lose her and for the rest of his life he would be alone.

The last night, when the *Sea-Serpent*, after steaming across the Ionian Sea, had entered the Corinthian Gulf, Lord Warburton ordered his Chef to prepare a special dinner.

Afterwards, they sat talking for a long time, the servants having long before withdrawn.

The only light came from the candles on the table as

the first glimmer of the stars in the sky overhead began to appear.

"To-morrow you will see your father, Corena . . ." Lord Warburton began.

He noticed because he was very observant of everything about her that her eyes seemed to light up for an instant, only to be replaced by a sudden darkness he could not comprehend.

"Do you think he will be at the port to meet you?" he went on.

Corena made a helpless little gesture with her hand as she answered hesitatingly:

"I . . . I do not . . . know . . . there may be . . . somebody . . . to tell me . . . where he is."

"It is unlikely if he is very ill that he will still be in Delphi," Lord Warburton persisted. "Where did your informant tell you he was staying when he came to your house?"

"He . . . he just told me . . . Papa was . . . very ill and . . . needed me."

The words seemed to be dragged from Corena's lips.

Although Lord Warburton knew it was distressing her to speak of it, he felt he had to know more.

"Wherever your father is," he said, "I will take you to him as comfortably and as quickly as possible."

"Thank . . . you."

"What I cannot understand," he continued, "is who will be tending him, or, if he is better, how he will be aware that you have arrived in Crisa."

The question was unanswerable, and therefore Corena said quickly:

"Please . . . do not let us . . . talk of it to-night. It is so . . . upsetting, and we will have the . . . answer to all these . . . questions . . . to-morrow."

There was a little pause before she said in a tone in which he could hear an unmistakable tremor of fear:

"What time . . . do we . . . arrive?"

"I have already instructed the Captain," he replied, "that to-night we will sleep in some quiet harbour inside the Corinthian Gulf."

He paused and went on:

"We will therefore reach Crisa in the morning, say about ten o'clock, when I hope you will receive good news of your father."

"What will . . . you . . . do?"

Lord Warburton's eyes were on her face as he replied:

"That depends, of course, how much you need me, and if there is anything I can do to help you."

The way he spoke made her draw in her breath.

Then once again they were looking into each other's eyes and it was impossible to look away.

As if she were afraid that the silence between them was more eloquent than words, Corena rose from the table.

Instinctively, she walked out on deck and Lord War- burton followed her.

She went to the railing, and now the last glimmer of the sun had vanished over the horizon.

The stars were growing brighter every minute and being reflected in the smooth sea.

There was a silence, then Corena looked up at the sky and said:

"I can see . . . Orion and he is very . . . bright to-night almost . . . as if he is shining . . . especially for . . . you!"

Lord Warburton knew she was talking so as to break the tension between them, and he said very quietly:

"It is for you that he is shining!"

He thought, although he was not certain, that a little tremor ran through her before she asked:

"You are . . . so strong . . . so clever . . . no one could really . . . hurt you . . . could they?"

He wondered at the question, but he replied:

"Being hurt physically is one thing; there are many far more subtle and cruel ways of being hurt."

He was thinking of the love that was burning in him because Corena was so near to him.

He thought perhaps he was a fool not to put his arms around her and tell her how much it would hurt him if she refused his love.

He thought she had not understood what he was trying to say, and after a moment he went on:

"I think, Corena, we have had an entirely unique experience in being together these past days. Will you miss me once you are with your father?"

There was a little pause before Corena replied:

"I shall . . . miss our . . . conversations . . . I never knew it was possible to talk to . . . any man as I have been able to . . . talk to you."

"Will you miss anything else?" he asked.

He wanted her to say that she would miss him. Instead, she answered:

"Y-you have opened up new . . . horizons for my mind . . . and made me understand things I have . . . never been able to understand before . . . and whether I see Greece to-morrow or not . . . I know it will . . . always be in my . . . heart."

She spoke in the same quiet, almost angelic tones that she used when she was speaking of the Oracle at Delphi.

Once again Lord Warburton felt she had slipped away from him and he could not hold her.

"There is something I want to say to you, Corena—" he replied.

Before he could say any more, she interrupted him.

"I must go . . . to . . . bed," she said. "There will be many . . . things to do . . . to-morrow . . . and perhaps I will . . . have to give . . . some of my . . . strength to my father."

He knew she was thinking that like those who took part in the Games, she needed the same vigour and strength to support her.

She did not wait for Lord Warburton to agree or disagree that she should leave him.

Instead, she said very quietly:

"Perhaps . . . to-morrow I shall be able to . . . thank you for all your . . . kindness to me . . . but to-night it is impossible . . . to find the . . . words."

Her voice quivered and he had the feeling that she was very near to tears.

But why? Why?

Why was it not possible for her to tell him what was wrong, even at the very last minute, so that he might help her?

He put out his hand as if to stop her from leaving, but it was too late.

As if it were a dream in which she moved away from him before he could realise what was happening, she had managed to slip away.

He was left alone with the sea and the sky and the despairing feeling that after to-morrow he might lose her forever.

When finally he went to his own cabin, he tried to tell himself his fears were unfounded and he was being absurd.

When he saw Sir Priam, and if it was necessary took

him in his yacht to Naples, from where he could travel by train back to England, he would tell him what he felt about Corena.

Then, of course, all the difficulties which lay between them to which he could not put a name would vanish.

He knew that one of the reasons he had been so careful not to upset Corena by telling her of his love was that he felt honour-bound to respect her because she was travelling on his yacht without a chaperone.

It was not of his contriving.

At the same time, he felt obligated towards anyone so young and, as he knew, pure and unsophisticated.

Yet his whole body burned with his love and all the devils of hell tempted him before he went below.

He had only to open the door of her cabin, and perhaps if he told her when she was in bed she would understand.

Then there would be the light he sometimes thought he saw in her eyes—the light of love.

"She loves me, I know she loves me!" he told himself, but he could not be sure.

Once again despair swept over him, and he found himself thinking of the words of Pindar:

And yet the hopes of man
Now ride on high, now are sunk low,
Cleaving their way through seas of false illusion.

Was the illusion false?

The question seemed almost to be shouted at him.

He knew the only person who could give the answer was Corena, who was in the next cabin to him.

When Hewlett had left him, being aware that his

Master had no wish to talk, Lord Warburton opened the port-hole in his cabin.

He drew back the curtains and let the light of the moon, which was now high in the sky, flood in.

Inevitably it made him think of Corena and he felt as if she came towards him, as Aphrodite might have done, on a shaft of moonlight.

Then, finding the beauty of the night, because it was hers, was almost unbearable, he forced himself to get into bed.

He thought it unlikely he would be able to sleep.

The *Sea-Serpent* was already at anchor, and there was only a very faint lap of the waves against her sides, and the silence of the night seemed to speak to him of his love.

"Oh, God, how can I win her?" he asked.

He knew as the words burst from his lips that Charles would laugh and say that this was what he had always wanted him to feel.

*   *   *

In her own cabin Corena was tossing from side to side in her bed.

She knew that she had so nearly betrayed herself to Lord Warburton when he stood beside her on deck under the stars.

She had to fight against an almost uncontrollable impulse to tell him how frightened she was of what was awaiting him at Crisa.

She mistrusted Mr. Thespidos's promises, and he hovered over her like some great vulture from which there was no escape.

"I . . . have to save Papa . . . I have to!" she said over

and over again as if to reassure herself she was doing the right thing.

Then, as the night seemed to deepen around her and everything was very quiet, she knew that to sacrifice Lord Warburton to Mr. Thespidos was a crime against everything in which she believed, everything which had been beautiful and holy to her ever since she had been a child.

It was not as Orion that she was thinking of him, but as Apollo, the god who was part of Greece itself, who had swum ashore at Crisa, where they would be to-morrow morning.

He had brought light to the whole world.

The Greeks had worshipped him and, she thought, she could understand how Apollo must have looked to them, very much like the magnificence of Lord Warburton.

She had never in her life enjoyed anything so much as being with him, talking to him, and listening to what he had to tell her.

At first it had been like being with her father.

Then she knew it was different, not only because Lord Warburton was the most handsome man she had ever seen, but also because he was young.

Although she tried to deny it, there was a vibration between them that was not explainable in words, but as if they spoke to each other in the language of the gods.

He was so strong, so fine, and at the same time so perceptive and understanding that she knew it would be hard to leave him.

Then suddenly, and she had not thought of this before, she realised that when she did so, he would loathe and despise her for handing him over as a hostage to Mr. Thespidos.

It had not occurred to her before that he would despise her and would never wish to set eyes on her again because she had betrayed him.

"He will understand . . . of course he will . . . understand that I had to . . . save Papa," she told herself.

Then she went on:

"Mr. Thespidos will ask an enormous ransom from him, and when he has paid it, he will go free."

It was then she remembered the evil expression on Mr. Thespidos's face.

Almost as if somebody were telling her so, she was aware that he would not be content just with money.

He would want to humiliate Lord Warburton, perhaps by taking from him not only his money, but his treasures, everything Greek that he had collected over the years.

She wanted to cry out at the idea of it, then even more frightening, that even that would not be enough.

Mr. Thespidos might want to torture him, just for the amusement of it, just to prove that Lord Warburton could suffer as any man would when he was helpless.

"I . . . I cannot . . . bear it!" Corena said to herself.

Almost as if she were being talked to by voices which filled the cabin, she put her hands over her ears and hid her face in the pillow.

"I have . . . to save Papa . . . I must . . . save Papa!"

She was speaking the words aloud even though they were stifled.

She could hear Mr. Thespidos say that if she betrayed him, if Lord Warburton was aware of what she was doing, her father would die, and not pleasantly.

She felt she could hear him screaming in agony and wanted to scream, too, but her voice died in her throat.

If it was not her father who screamed, it would be Lord Warburton!

It was then as she thought of him suffering that she knew, as she had known for days, that she loved him more than anything else on earth.

She loved his clear-cut features, the height and breadth of his forehead, the squareness of his chin.

She loved the sensitivity of his hands, the breadth of his shoulders, and the athletic movement of his body.

She loved the deepness in his voice when he spoke to her and the way certain things he said made her quiver inside almost as if they lit a flame.

"I love him!" she said despairingly.

Not really realising what she was doing, she got out of bed to go to the port-hole.

It was open to let in the cool night air.

As she pulled back the curtains she could see the constellation of Orion shining above her.

Orion, Apollo, whichever he was, he was a god and she dared not destroy him.

No shelter has Apollo, nor sacred laurel leaves;
The fountains now are silent; the voice is stilled.

The words seemed to be whispered in the lap of the sea.

She knew that if Lord Warburton died at the hands of Mr. Thespidos, it would be she who had really killed him.

He was the God of Light whom the whole world, whether they knew it or not, worshipped.

She shut her eyes.

Then, looking up at the stars, she thought they were

telling her what she must do and she dared not disobey them.

Without thinking, driven by a feeling of urgency, of terror, and at the same time of love, she opened her cabin door.

Everything was quiet and dark as she turned the handle of Lord Warburton's door and went inside.

He was awake, thinking of Corena and his love, and suddenly he was aware that she was standing only a few feet from him.

The moonlight illuminated her hair as it flowed over her shoulders onto the diaphanous nightgown she wore.

It flashed through his mind that he was seeing a vision of Aphrodite herself, and she had come to him.

Then with a little cry Corena ran towards the bed and dropped down on her knees.

"I have ... to tell ... you!" she said in a quick, breathless, terrified little voice. "You ... are in ... danger! To-morrow a man will be ... waiting for you but ... I cannot do it! I know ... now that I ... cannot do it!"

Her voice broke and the tears seemed to choke her.

"What are you saying to me, Corena?" Lord Warburton asked. "What are you telling me?"

"H-he said ... if I did not ... come with you to ... Crisa ... he would ... kill Papa ... and I know that he has ... already ... tortured him!"

She fought for breath as she added:

"Now ... he will ... do it ... to you!"

It was impossible to say any more as the tears came, and she put her face down on the bed and sobbed bitterly, the sound breaking the silence and seeming to become part of the moonlight.

She cried despairingly, all the pent-up horror of the

last weeks seeping through her so that she could no longer think.

She could only feel that she was already a murderess, killing both her father and Lord Warburton, whom she loved.

She did not realise that he had slipped out of bed on the other side, put on a dark robe that Hewlett had left on a chair, and come round to where she was kneeling.

He bent down and very gently picked her up in his arms.

She was still crying helplessly and uncontrollably.

As he sat down on the bed and cradled her against him, she went on weeping against his shoulder.

He held her very close and, although she was not aware of it, his lips were on the softness of her hair.

Then he said:

"Stop crying, my darling, and tell me what all this is about."

Because his voice was so quiet and yet so firm, it percolated through her misery.

While the tears still flowed, they were not so tempestuous.

She could feel the strength of his arms and was conscious that she was close to him and that for the moment she felt safe, protected, and the terror of Mr. Thespidos had receded a little.

Gently, so very gently that she could hardly realise it was happening, Lord Warburton put his fingers under her chin and turned her face up to his.

In the moonlight he could see very clearly.

The tears were running down her cheeks, her lips were trembling, and her wet eye-lashes were dark as she closed her eyes because she dared not look at him.

For one moment he looked at her, then his lips were on hers.

As she felt them, it was not even a shock to Corena. It was as if everything that was happening was inevitable, and had been decreed since the beginning of time.

At first his kiss was gentle and very tender, because he comforted her.

Then, as if the softness and innocence of her lips made him more sure of himself, the pressure increased.

He kissed her demandingly, possessively, as if he made her his.

It was then that Corena knew this was what she had been longing for, although she had not been aware of it.

She felt her whole being move towards him and become a part of him.

She thought wildly it was something she should not do, but she gave him her heart, her soul, and herself.

Now she was no longer alone and frightened, but his.

He kissed her and at last her tears abated.

Then, as she opened her eyes the stars shone above his head, he was no longer human, but Orion, and they were both part of the sky and one with the gods.

"I love you!" Corena whispered, and it did not seem wrong to say it.

Love pulsated through her so that she could no longer think clearly, but only feel.

"As I love you!" Lord Warburton said. "My darling, how could you have tortured me by making me feel I might lose you?"

He did not wait for an answer but was kissing her again, kissing her fiercely, demandingly, as if he defied the whole world to take her from him.

It was so perfect, so wonderful, Corena could be

aware only that the stars were not around them alone, but within her, shining within her breast.

Then with a little cry of horror she came back to reality.

"Y-you . . . do not understand," she said, "you . . . must listen to . . . me!"

"My precious, my darling, my wonderful little Aphrodite," Lord Warburton said, "nothing matters except that you love me as I love you."

He would have kissed her again, but with an effort she turned her face aside.

"I have to tell you," she said, "then . . . perhaps you will . . . no longer . . . love me."

Lord Warburton smiled at the absurdity of such an idea, then he said:

"I am listening, my lovely one. At the same time, I find it impossible not to kiss you when for these last days you have driven me nearly mad! I have never, and this is true, felt so frustrated in my whole life!"

"I thought . . . I could do what was . . . wrong and . . . wicked," Corena said, "but now I know that it is . . . impossible . . . yet how can I allow them to . . . kill Papa?"

Now the agony was back in her voice and Lord Warburton heard it.

He drew her a little closer to him before he said:

"Tell me about it, my precious, and do not be afraid."

"B-but . . . I am afraid!"

There was a little pause. Then she said in a voice he could hardly hear:

"When you . . . know what I have . . . done . . . you will stop . . . loving me."

"That is impossible! We have loved each other since

135

the beginning of time," Lord Warburton said, "and nothing you can do or say now could prevent me from worshipping you for the rest of eternity!"

Corena gave a little sob and turned her face against his shoulder.

"Tell me," he said, "I know you have been hiding some momentous secret which you would not share with me."

Hesitating, stumbling over her words, and with the tears once again running down her cheeks, Corena told him how Mr. Thespidos had come to the house, how he told her there was only one way she could save her father.

She hesitated for a long time before she said:

"H-he said I had to try and . . . attract you in . . . wicked . . . horrible words. That is why . . . when I came to . . . see you at your house . . . I wore Papa's spectacles . . . so that you would not . . . think me . . . attractive."

"I might have known," Lord Warburton answered, "there was no escape for either of us."

Corena went on to tell him how Mr. Thespidos had told her she had to be a stowaway and how he had drugged her with the coffee she had drunk.

After that she had known nothing until she woke up aboard the *Sea-Serpent*.

The way she spoke and the way she hid her face against him told Lord Warburton everything he wanted to know.

He knew now why there had been a barrier between them.

Because of what Mr. Thespidos suggested, Corena had been terrified of attracting him as a woman, as it would seem vulgar and improper.

There was a tender expression in his eyes that had never been there before as he said:

"My darling, all that matters is that now you have told me, I can somehow contrive to extract your father from the clutches of this monstrous Greek!

"B-but he may . . . kill you . . . or torture you!"

"And that would worry you?"

"I love you . . . I love you . . . I do not believe it . . . but I cannot help loving you. How could I do anything so . . . wicked as to hurt . . . Apollo?"

The words were slightly indistinct, but Lord Warburton heard them.

"I am very proud, my darling," he said, "to be Apollo, and if you think of me as the God of Light, then I must live up to my name, and it is something I have every intention of doing."

"B-but . . . suppose . . . suppose he seizes and . . . hurts you?"

"That, my precious, is where you will have to trust me," Lord Warburton said. "I know, because I love you, I shall 'slay the dragon' and both your father and I will be free."

"You must be careful . . . very, very careful!" Corena warned.

"Trust me," Lord Warburton said. "I wish only that you had been brave enough to tell me this before now."

"We are . . . not too . . . late?"

Again the fear was there and Lord Warburton turned her face up to his and kissed her very gently.

"If I am a god," he said, "you have to believe in me. As you are the Goddess of Love, I know, my darling, the gods themselves will look after and protect you."

It seemed to Corena as he spoke that he glowed with a special light that came from Heaven itself.

Because she wanted to believe him and his arms were very comforting, she surrendered herself to his kisses.

She tried not to think of what would happen to-morrow.

*   *   *

A long time later, Lord Warburton said:

"Now, my beautiful darling, I am going to send you to bed. I want you to sleep for what is left of the night, and to help me to-morrow by giving me strength and courage in what I have to do."

"I . . . will try," Corena said meekly.

He rose to his feet, still holding her in his arms, and carried her from his cabin into hers.

He put her gently down on the bed.

He realised as he did so that she had not given a thought to the fact that she had been in his arms wearing only her thin nightgown.

In her innocence and purity and her lack of self-consciousness it had never occurred to her while they were concerned with much more important and greater things.

At the same time, he knew that few women would have felt as she did, and none of those he had known in the past would have offered him their souls.

"I adore you, my little Aphrodite!" he said.

He pulled the sheets over her.

In the moonlight it was difficult still to believe she was real and not, as he had first thought, a stone sculpture of the goddess he had always sought.

Her lips were warm, and as he felt them quiver beneath his, he knew no one could be more human, more exciting, or more adorable.

"Good-night, my lovely one," he said. "After to-morrow we shall be together. There will be no more dragons, only the love that you give to the whole world."

He kissed her again, then went from the cabin as if he were forcing himself to leave her and it was very hard.

Only when he had gone did Corena shut her eyes and say over and over again:

"Thank You . . . God, and please . . . protect him . . . keep him safe . . . and save Papa . . . I cannot . . . lose them."

She prayed, and went on praying with an intensity which came from the very depths of her heart, until from sheer exhaustion she fell asleep.

chapter seven

CORENA was awoken by Hewlett coming into the room.

Instantly she sat up, afraid because she had been asleep that something had happened and she was not aware of it.

"'Morning! Miss!" Hewlett said in his usual hearty manner. "'Is Lordship says there's no 'urry and we shan't be movin' into 'arbour for another hour."

Corena did not answer but merely lay back, feeling very limp against her pillows.

It was not only the exhaustion of her tears the night before, it was a feeling of helplessness.

It was as if she were being carried along on a tidal wave and nothing she could do or say would stop it.

Then she remembered that Lord Warburton had said that he loved her, and she felt the words glow inside her as if the sunshine were burning in her heart.

"I love . . . him! I . . . love him!" she whispered.

She hardly noticed Hewlett come out of the bathroom and leave her cabin without speaking.

It was unlike him, as he was usually so talkative.

However, she could think of nothing but that once she was dressed she would see Lord Warburton and be quite certain he really loved her.

Suppose last night had just been a dream?

No, she was certain it was true.

She dressed quickly, but took trouble in arranging her hair and put on one of her prettiest gowns.

She now wanted him to admire her; she wanted to be beautiful for him.

But when she looked in the mirror she was aware that her eyes were frightened and she was very pale.

The yacht had not moved from where they had anchored last night, but when she was dressed and ready to go to the Saloon for breakfast, she heard the engines start up.

She thought they were moving slowly and knew it could not be slow enough, because she was so afraid of what she would find when they reached Crisa.

She went into the Saloon and, as she expected, Lord Warburton was already there.

He was standing by the windows looking out at the land, and for a moment he was not aware of her presence.

Then, as if she drew him by her thoughts and her love, he turned round and they stood just looking as if they had never seen each other before.

With a little cry Corena ran towards him to fling herself into his arms.

"It is true . . . tell me it is . . . true!" she begged.

"That I love you?" he asked.

He was smiling, and she thought she had never seen him look so happy.

Then the fear that grew within her made her say frantically:

"I love you . . . but I am afraid . . . desperately . . . afraid that he . . . may hurt you."

He held her very tightly.

"I told you to trust me."

He kissed her and it was a gentle, tender kiss, as if he dedicated himself to looking after and protecting her.

She thought as his lips held her captive that her agitation subsided and, although it seemed impossible, that he would save her father and himself.

Lord Warburton released her and said quietly:

"Now, my darling, you have to eat a good breakfast and, while you do so, you will remember that we are nearing the place where Apollo landed, the 'Shining Cliffs,' which we will look at together, above him."

Corena sat down at the table, and, because she knew it would please him, tried to eat what was put in front of her.

While she did so, Lord Warburton went on speaking of Apollo and his constant companion, "the sleekest and shiniest of all creatures, the dolphin."

To Corena it was as if she were a child again and her father was telling her stories of Greece.

Even when she was very small she had found them more absorbing than fairy-stories.

Only when she had drunk her coffee and actually eaten quite a lot of what was on her plate was she aware that the yacht was moving into harbour.

She drew in her breath, feeling that the Dragon was not waiting beyond the olive groves where Apollo had found him, but would be on the Quayside.

Like a knife turning in a wound, she remembered the end of the lines from Homer that she and Lord Warburton had quoted to each other:

> *Make the sky clear, and grant us to see with*
> *our eyes.*
> *In the light be it, though thou slayest me.*

She felt the words burning their way into her consciousness like fire.

> *Though thou slayest me!*

Supposing Mr. Thespidos slew them all—her father, Lord Warburton, and herself?

She wanted to scream at the idea, then was even more afraid that if he slew the two men, she would be left alive.

She had not forgotten the way he had looked at her.

She knew he had made the insinuations about attracting Lord Warburton because she attracted him also, a thought which sickened her.

She had not told Lord Warburton that she loathed Mr. Thespidos as a man.

He had, however, read her thoughts, and he put his arms around her as she rose from the table and said:

"I love you, my adorable goddess, and no other man shall ever touch you or insult you by his attentions. You are mine, completely and absolutely mine!"

Corena turned her cheek against his shoulder.

"That is . . . what I . . . want to . . . be," she whispered.

"That is what you will be," he said, "but Dragons have to be attended to first!"

She tried to laugh, but her voice broke on a tear and he said:

"I am expecting you to be brave. Remember that I find in you 'every sweet thing, be it wisdom, beauty or glory, makes rich the soul of man.'"

Corena gave a little sob as she listened to Pindar's words.

It was what she wanted him to feel about her, and knew that she must not disappoint him by not living up to them.

The yacht took what seemed a long time, moving slowly with the land on either side of it towards the Quayside at the end.

It was a day of sunshine, but there was a freshness in the air that seemed somehow different from anything Corena had ever smelt before.

She knew, too, that the light on the land and in the sky was the light that the Greeks were never tired of describing.

She tried not to think of the man who was waiting for them in Crisa.

Instead, she remembered the Greeks believed that the body of Apollo poured across the sky.

Intensely virile, flashing with a million points of light, healing everything he touched, he defied the powers of darkness.

If Lord Warburton was Apollo, then Mr. Thespidos was the power of darkness.

As she gave a little shudder at the thought of him, she looked up at Lord Warburton and thought that not even Apollo could be more handsome than he was.

She felt in a strange way that he exuded the power, the determination, and the vibrations of the god with whom she identified him.

He had been looking out at the land they were passing, the rocks of which seemed bare but were gleaming in the morning light.

Now he looked down at Corena and said very gently:

"Believe in me! I need your faith as well as your love!"

"It is . . . yours! It is yours . . . completely!" Corena cried. "And I . . . love you until I can . . . think of nothing else . . . except of . . . course Papa."

There was a little tremor on the last words, and Lord Warburton said:

"He will be thinking of you, and I cannot believe that like us he is not trusting in the gods to protect him."

"Of course Papa will be . . . doing . . . that!"

Lord Warburton led her to the sofa, and they sat down side by side.

"There is no hurry," he said, "everything has been planned and all you have to do, my precious little Aphrodite, is to obey me and try to appear unafraid."

"What . . . are you . . . asking?" Corena said quickly.

"When the ship is tied up, I want you to go down the gangway to where I am almost sure you will see your father waiting for you on the Quay."

He looked at her for a moment to see if she was listening, then went on:

"You will throw your arms around him, as I know you will want to do anyway, and kiss him."

Corena was listening intently as he continued:

"In your left hand I want you to carry a present for him which you will hold up excitedly so that everybody can see it."

"A . . . a present?" Corena asked in a puzzled tone.

"Put it into your father's right hand," Lord Warburton

said as if she had not spoken, "then keep close beside him."

"And . . . what will . . . you be . . . doing?"

"I shall be waiting, my precious, to slay the Dragon and save your father!"

He bent his head with the last words and kissed her so that she could not reply.

Although she wanted to go on asking him questions, she knew he did not wish to say any more, and she was determined to please him.

Only when he heard the engines stop did Lord Warburton rise to his feet.

"Wait here!" he said, and it was a command.

He walked across the Saloon and Corena knew that without being seen himself he was looking out through the glass door which led out onto the deck.

She knew he would be able to see the Quay where they had tied up.

Because there was very little noise, Corena was certain they were moored where there were no sight-seers, and, she suspected, although she was not sure, few other vessels.

Lord Warburton stood without moving for some minutes. Then he came back to say:

"I think, my darling, your father is waiting for you."

Corena jumped to her feet and Lord Warburton said sternly:

"Move slowly and carry your present for him as I told you to do."

Abashed, because for the moment she had forgotten it, Corena picked it up from the table. It was wrapped in white tissue paper and tied with a large bow of red ribbon.

Then, as she held it in her hand, she knew it was a

revolver and looked enquiringly at Lord Warburton.

"Your father may need it," he said very quietly. "Hand it to him so that as he takes it he grasps the handle."

"Yes . . . yes . . . of course."

She was very pale, but he loved the way she lifted her chin proudly, as if she would not let whoever was waiting for them on the Quay see how frightened she was.

Lord Warburton took her hand in his and drew her out of the Saloon, and just before he opened the glass door onto the deck, he said:

"The gods go with you, my beautiful darling."

She managed to smile at him.

Then, as she went to the gangway, she saw he had been right and her father was on the Quay.

He was standing a little way back from the yacht, and there was a dark-haired man close behind him who she knew instinctively was his jailor.

Much nearer to the *Sea-Serpent* was Mr. Thespidos.

He was alone, but one quick glance told Corena there were four other men guarding her father.

They were standing in the background but watching everything in what she thought was a threatening manner, their right hands in the pockets of the coats they were wearing.

She drew in her breath.

Then with the pride she knew Lord Warburton expected, she began slowly to descend the gangway, holding up her present.

A slight breeze from the sea fluttered the red ribbon with which it was tied.

She was aware that Lord Warburton was behind her.

When she stepped on land, she ran to her father, crying out as she did so:

"Papa . . . Papa! I am . . . here!"

She flung her arms around his neck, at the same time pushing the revolver into his right hand.

She felt his fingers close over it.

Then as she kissed him she said, her words falling over themselves:

"How are . . . you? You are . . . not ill? Oh . . . Papa . . . I have . . . missed you so . . . terribly!"

"As I have missed you," her father said, and she knew the words came fervently from his lips.

She saw then that he was very pale and there were lines under his eyes as if he were ill. He also looked very much thinner than when she had last seen him.

It was only a quick impression, for at that moment Lord Warburton must have descended the gangway and she heard Mr. Thespidos say:

"Good-morning, Mr Lord! I have great pleasure in welcoming you to Greece!"

He was sneering, and Corena could hear it in his voice.

"I do not think," Lord Warburton replied haughtily, "that we have met before."

"My name is Thespidos. I am here to inform you that you are now my prisoner!"

"Your prisoner?" Lord Warburton exclaimed in apparent surprise. "I think you must be mistaken!"

"No, My Lord, and let me say quite clearly so that you understand that unless you come with me quietly and without any fuss, Sir Priam Melville, who has just been greeted by his daughter, will die!"

Mr. Thespidos was speaking in the gloating, oily way which had frightened Corena before.

Now, as he drew a revolver from his pocket and pointed it at Lord Warburton, Corena, by a supreme effort of will, did not scream in fear.

Instead, she only held on to her father.

She was aware as she did so that the man behind him was holding not a revolver in his hand, but one of the long, sharp, deadly knives which could kill a man with a single thrust.

He had the point of it against her father's back.

He was, however, watching the interchange between Lord Warburton and Mr. Thespidos with a smirk on his face.

Although Lord Warburton seemed to tower above the Greek, Corena thought in horror that he was unarmed.

She wondered frantically how he could have been so foolish as to come ashore without any protection.

She wondered whether, if she ran towards him, she would be able to throw herself between him and Mr. Thespidos.

Then she was aware of the other men who were standing back and who she was certain either had a revolver or a knife in their pockets.

A streak of agony ran through her body as she thought there was nothing any of them could do except watch Mr. Thespidos take Lord Warburton away.

Then Lord Warburton said, still in the tone he had used before:

"Are you threatening me, my good man?"

"Perhaps I should explain to you a little more fully and in a more private place," Mr. Thespidos replied. "If Your Lordship will kindly walk in through the open door just ahead of you without making any trouble, I will allow Miss Melville to take her father aboard your yacht."

Without seeing his face, Corena knew that Mr. Thespidos was smiling his evil smile at the success of his plan.

She was suddenly aware there was a small open door in the high wall behind her father which she had not noticed before.

She knew that once Mr. Thespidos had Lord Warburton inside, he and his men would render him powerless.

Then they would take him to some secret place where they had perhaps imprisoned her father.

She felt she could not bear it, could not allow it to happen. Yet what could she do?

She wanted to run to Lord Warburton's side, and at the same time to plead with Mr. Thespidos to take anything, even his yacht, if he would spare him.

Then, as it appeared that Lord Warburton was about to do what Mr. Thespidos ordered, he took a step forward as if to move towards the open door, but as he did so he swung round.

With the punch of an expert pugilist he caught the Greek a blow on the chin which knocked him backwards onto the ground with a crash.

His revolver clattered to the ground as he did so.

As his men reached into their pockets for the weapons they carried, a dozen seamen appeared at the railings on the deck of the *Sea-Serpent* with rifles pointing directly at the Greeks below them.

Corena gasped at what was happening.

Then, as she thought the man behind her father was about to press the knife into his body, Sir Priam moved suddenly and shot him in the arm.

The sound seemed to reverberate in the clear air and, as it did so, Mr. Thespidos's men turned to run, but they were too late.

At the end of the Quay a number of Policemen appeared, led by Hewlett.

The men hesitated, and were lost.

The Policemen ran forward and seized the four of them.

The man who had been shot by Sir Priam tried, clutching his arm which was dripping with blood, to reach the door in the wall, only to find as he did so two other Policemen waiting there.

It was then that Corena, although she was not aware of it, with tears running down her cheeks, clung to her father and he said gently:

"Thank you, my dearest, I might have guessed that you would be clever enough to save me."

"It-it was . . . Lord Warburton . . ." she murmured, but he was not listening.

Instead, he walked to where Lord Warburton was standing waiting for the Policemen to remove the unconscious Mr. Thespidos.

Sir Priam held out his hand.

"How can I thank you for coming to my rescue and being so extremely clever about it?"

"Are you all right?" Lord Warburton asked.

"A little the worse for wear, and very hungry," Sir Priam replied with a wry smile.

"Oh . . . Papa . . . have they been . . . starving . . . you?" Corena asked.

"They were the most unpleasant criminals it was ever my misfortune to encounter," Sir Priam replied, "and I can only thank God you are here!"

Lord Warburton looked at Corena.

"Take your father aboard and feed him," he said. "I must speak to the Police about these men, then I will join you."

Corena followed her father aboard, and only when he sat down at the table in the Saloon did she realise how different he looked from when she had last seen him.

"Have . . . they been very . . . cruel to you, Papa?" she faltered.

"I will tell you about it later," Sir Priam answered. "All I want at the moment is something to eat and drink. It is a long time since I have had either."

A steward hurried away to the galley to bring him eggs and bacon, hot toast and coffee.

It took a little time, and because she could not help herself, Corena went to the window to see if Lord Warburton was really safe.

She could see him talking to a man who was obviously a Senior Police Officer, and everybody else had left.

After a long conversation the Officer saluted and Lord Warburton began to come up the gangway.

Because she was afraid he might think she was spying on him, Corena went back to the table.

Her father was already eating as if he had never seen food before.

Then, as Lord Warburton came into the Saloon, her eyes met his and it was impossible to think of anything but their love.

* * *

Very much later in the day, after Sir Priam had rested, he was able to tell them a little of what he had undergone at the hands of Mr. Thespidos.

He made his story amusing, but Corena knew that he was making light of what had been a horrifying experience so that she should not be too upset.

"He was absolutely convinced that I had found the

statue of Aphrodite, which you, too, are seeking," Sir Priam said.

"And did you find it?" Lord Warburton asked.

Sir Priam took a sip of the very excellent champagne which had swept away his pallor before he answered:

"Yes, I have!"

Corena gave a little cry of delight.

"Oh, Papa, how wonderful! But you did not . . . tell them?"

"They tortured me most unpleasantly," Sir Priam replied, "but I would not degrade myself by giving these felons something they intended to sell to any bidder who would fill their dirty pockets with gold."

"So they did not get the information from you?"

"No! They were finally convinced that the only person who really knew where Aphrodite could be found was Your Lordship!"

"They were quite right!" Lord Warburton said.

Corena looked at him in surprise.

"You do know?"

"I have found Aphrodite," Lord Warburton replied.

He put out his hand as he spoke to Corena, who placed hers in it.

Sir Priam looked from one to the other, then gave a little laugh.

"So that is what has been happening!"

"I love him, Papa," Corena said, "but I told him the truth about what was happening only last night. I was so desperately . . . afraid that if I did so Mr. Thespidos would . . . carry out his . . . threat to . . . kill you."

"He told me that is how he had threatened you," Sir Priam said. "I might have known that you, Warburton, would be clever enough to outwit him!"

"I could hardly allow my future father-in-law to die

so ignominiously," Lord Warburton replied.

Both men laughed, and Sir Priam raised his glass of champagne.

"To you both," he said, "and how, linked together by your love of Greece, could you be anything but very happy!"

Corena got up and kissed him.

Until Lord Warburton insisted that Sir Priam should go to bed and rest, they talked of Greece, its beauty, and its treasures, which to Corena seemed very much a part of her love.

Only when her father had gone to his cabin and she knew he was half asleep before Hewlett could help him undress did she say to Lord Warburton:

"Are we . . . leaving?"

He put his arms round her and said:

"I think we would be very faint-hearted if we left without taking your father's Aphrodite with us."

She looked at him in surprise and he said:

"I have you, my adorable little goddess, and I want nothing else, but I cannot allow your father to have suffered for nothing."

Corena drew in her breath before she said in a very small voice:

"Will you . . . both be safe?"

"Completely!" Lord Warburton replied. "Thespidos and his gang are now in custody, and will serve heavy sentences not only for this crime but for many others they have committed and for which they have not yet paid the penalty."

He saw she was still worried, and went on:

"When we go to look for your father's treasure, I will make sure that we are guarded by my own men as well as by the Police, who have already offered us their protection."

"You . . . think of . . . everything!" Corena murmured.

"I think of you because it is impossible to think of anything else."

He kissed her until the dozens of questions she had been wanting to ask him slipped away from her mind.

She was conscious of nothing but the closeness of his arms.

His lips carried her into the sky and made her feel as if she held the stars against her breast.

*   *   *

Early the following morning Lord Warburton was, Corena knew, giving orders on deck.

She wondered what he was planning, when he came into the Saloon where her father had just joined her.

"I feel a different man!" Sir Priam declared as he sat down at the table. "After the food I have been allowed these past weeks, I am now ready to eat the proverbial ox, or anything else Your Lordship cares to offer me!"

The stewards were smiling as they hurried in with half-a-dozen dishes.

There was fish fresh from the sea and lobsters that had been caught that morning.

Also several other dishes which Corena knew were Greek and unobtainable elsewhere because it was impossible to find the right fish.

When Lord Warburton came into the Saloon, Corena thought she had never seen him look so happy.

As if he could not help himself, he put his arms around her and kissed her cheek, saying as he did so:

"You look even more beautiful to-day than you did yesterday!"

"Yesterday I was frightened," Corena admitted, "but to-day I am safe in Greece with . . . you and Papa."

The way she spoke made both men smile at her, and as Lord Warburton sat down at the table, he said:

"I have something to suggest to you both, to which I hope you will agree."

Corena looked at him apprehensively.

She had a sudden fear that he would want to stay in Greece and send her and her father away on the *Sea-Serpent*.

"The Captain has been investigating for me in Crisa," he said, "and has found, as I hoped he would, a Christian Missionary who is spending his holiday visiting Delphi before he returns to Africa."

Corena was puzzled before he went on:

"I thought that nothing could be more appropriate, and I hope, Sir Priam, you will agree that Corena and I should be married in Delphi."

For a moment there was absolute silence. Then Corena gave a little cry of sheer joy.

"Do you mean it . . . do you really . . . mean it?"

"It is possible," Lord Warburton replied, "because every Missionary, as your father well knows, carries with him a consecrated stone."

He saw Corena did not understand and explained:

"This means that he can conduct marriages, baptise children, and give Holy Communion in any place, as long as the stone is with him."

He took Corena's hand in his as he said:

"We can be married in the Temple of Apollo or, if you prefer, my darling, which I think is more appropriate to you, the Temple of Athene."

"That, as it happens, would be very appropriate," Sir

Priam said, "for it is at Athene's Temple that I have found Aphrodite!"

"It is really there?" Lord Warburton exclaimed.

"It is, and I found it quite by chance just below the steps leading up to the base on which the Temple stood. Thousands of people must have passed by without realising where she was lying!"

"And when you found it, what happened?"

"I was aware, even as I uncovered the top of the head, that I was being watched," Sir Priam replied. "I was alone at dusk, and I realised it would be dangerous to dig any further."

"It was . . . Mr. Thespidos!" Corena said in a very low voice.

"It was one of his minions," Sir Priam corrected her, "but Mr. Thespidos was not far away. When I started to walk back to the village where I was staying that night, they seized me."

His voice sharpened as he went on:

"They carried me away to an isolated house where they had camped out so that they could prey on any Archaeologists who had discovered anything they thought could be valuable."

"The Policemen told me," Lord Warburton remarked, "that Thespidos himself is suspected of committing several murders when Archaeologists have tried to defend their findings."

Corena gave a little cry of horror, and her father said quietly:

"It is all right, my dearest. Thespidos will be in prison for very many years."

"I cannot bear to . . . think of you being in the . . . hands of that . . . terrible man!"

At the same time, she looked, as she spoke, at Lord

Warburton and knew that she was also thinking of what would have happened to him.

"What I have arranged," he said, as if he wished to change the subject, "is that the Missionary, who is eager to explore Delphi on his own, will meet us at the Temple of Athene at five o'clock, when the other sight-seers will have departed and we shall have the place to ourselves."

He saw the excitement in Corena's eyes and continued:

"What I would like to suggest, Sir Priam, is that when Corena and I are married we will go the small Hotel in the village, which I have taken over for the night."

Corena made a little murmur of happiness and looked so lovely as she did so that it was with an effort Lord Warburton went on to Sir Priam:

"Food will be waiting for you here in the yacht at whatever time you return, which I presume will be when my men have finished their digging under your supervision and Aphrodite had been carried aboard my yacht."

"I will be with them," Sir Priam said briefly.

"The walk will not be . . . too much for . . . you?" Corena asked.

"If it is, I will be comforted by Aphrodite on the return journey, and I shall feel too excited to be tired," Sir Priam said quietly.

"We will not have to walk," Lord Warburton said. "The horses I·have hired are, they assure me, the very best in Crisa, and as they have not made the journey for several days, they will be fresh when they carry us up early in the afternoon."

Corena drew in her breath.

"I cannot imagine a more...wonderful way of being...married!" she exclaimed.

"That is what I hoped you would say," Lord Warburton replied. "We will leave your father to be looked after by the Captain in the yacht, and we will be alone."

He did not emphasise the word, but the expression in his eyes was very revealing.

Because he had slept very little the night before, soon after luncheon Sir Priam went to lie down, and Corena did the same.

She fell asleep almost as soon as her head touched the pillow.

* * *

When Corena awoke she was saying a prayer of thankfulness for the blessings she had received.

Her father was alive and had found his Aphrodite, and she had found the Apollo of her dreams.

He was the man she had always imagined was somewhere in the world, but she might never be able to discover him.

The sun was not as hot as it had been as they set off up the winding path that led through the olive groves and up the steep hill towards Delphi.

Once they were out of the port, Corena could see very clearly the beetling rocks called the *Phaedriades* —the 'Shining Ones,' which she knew were always moist from the mountain springs.

They looked so lovely, and long before she saw the pillars and the ruins of Apollo's Temple she thought it was a suitable dwelling place for the god.

Even lovelier was the view when she looked down than when she had looked up.

Now she had the impression that the valley, the

mountains, and the sea were slowly revolving around the "Shining Cliffs," which reached a thousand feet above her head, implacably stern and remote.

When they moved away from the Temple of Apollo she could see a little below them the ruins of the Temple of Athene.

Its Doric pillars seemed in the last evening rays of the sun to rise and become whole again as when the Temple was one of the finest sights in Delphi.

It was not what she saw but what she felt that made Corena know that this was the supreme moment of her life.

She was loved and was marrying a man who was indivisibly joined in her mind with Apollo.

They left the horses behind and walked the short distance down from the Temple of Apollo to that of Athene.

It was then that they saw standing there, with his back to the three columns which remained unbroken, the Priest who was to marry them.

Behind him on one of the fallen pillars was his consecrated stone.

Corena had travelled up the hill on a comfortable saddle that Crisa provided for tourists.

It was more like a seat on the horse's back, and Lord Warburton had covered it with a white silk cloth.

This not only protected her gown but also made it even more comfortable than it would otherwise have been.

She did not have to bother with holding the reins in her hands because the horses were led.

She knew as Lord Warburton kept looking at her that in her white gown, which was simple but in exquisite taste, and with a shady hat which protected her skin from the sun, she looked very bridal.

When they reached Delphi she left her hat with the horses and put a wreath of real white flowers on her head.

Lord Warburton had also provided her with a small bouquet of white flowers to carry in her hand.

As she and her father ascended the steps of the platform, Lord Warburton moved ahead of them so that he was waiting in front of the Priest.

It was then, as the Service began, that Corena felt that from the "Shining Cliffs" above them there were not only the eagles soaring overhead, but the gods themselves, who had come to be present at her marriage.

She could feel the vibrations from them.

She was sure, too, when she and Lord Warburton knelt and the Priest blessed them, there was a strange light shining on the top of the Temple and enveloping them with its glory.

She knew it was the light of Apollo and that they had received not only the blessing of God in whom they both believed, but the blessing, too, of the gods of Greece.

It was nearly dark by the time they left Sir Priam with the seamen who were to dig for him at the Temple of Athene.

The Missionary had returned to wherever he came from, and Corena was alone in the little Hotel with Lord Warburton.

She had found that the Sitting-Room waiting for them was massed with flowers, which had been picked in the fields around Delphi and came, too, she thought, from the market-place in Crisa.

They scented the air and made the plain little room a bower of beauty.

There was food which had been cooked by Lord Warburton's Chef from the *Sea-Serpent*.

The champagne seemed as golden as the sun that had shone on them as they rode up the long steep path to Delphi as many thousands of pilgrims had done before them.

Corena knew the gods were still with them, and she was very conscious of them in the silences which fell between her and Lord Warburton.

Her heart spoke to his heart and it was impossible to translate what was being said into ordinary words.

"Papa is so happy," she managed to say.

"Very happy," Lord Warburton replied, "and he told me before we left him he will not be joining us on the yacht."

Corena looked surprised and Lord Warburton explained:

"He knows we want to be alone and he wishes to go on searching for a month to find more treasures."

"He . . . will be . . . safe?"

"I will leave two of my best men with him."

Corena gave a little sigh and replied:

"You are so . . . kind."

"I am selfish," Lord Warburton replied, "because I want you, my beautiful, precious wife, to myself."

When the stewards who had waited on them left the room, they were alone.

The stars were coming out in the sky above them, and Lord Warburton put his arms around Corena and said:

"It has been a long day, my darling, but I feel it is one we shall always remember."

"How could I ever forget . . . anything so . . . wonderful as . . . marrying you in the . . . Temple of Athene?"

Corena dropped her voice because she was shy as she said:

"I was . . . sure as we prayed that the . . . gods had come to the . . . marriage of . . . Apollo."

"And I knew," Lord Warburton said, "that I had found the real Aphrodite, the Goddess of Love! That is you, my precious, and you will never die because you will live in everyone who ever falls in love!"

Corena turned her lips up to his, but he did not kiss them.

Instead, he looked down at her and asked:

"How can you be so perfect, so beautiful, and at the same time a real woman?"

Then as her heart leapt at the words, he said fiercely:

"You are my woman—mine completely and absolutely, and I will never lose you, never let you go! We were joined together by the gods, and as gods we will live and love for eternity."

"That is . . . what I . . . want to do . . . and . . . oh . . . darling, I love you so completely that it is . . . impossible to tell . . . you how . . . much!"

"Why try?" Lord Warburton asked.

He drew her very gently from the Sitting-Room across the narrow landing into the bed-room.

She realised that here, too, he had transformed a quite ordinary room with flowers.

There was a large bed which had been carved by Greek craftsmen and painted with flowers and animals.

The sheets bore Lord Warburton's insignia and the pillows were edged with lace. There were white fur rugs on the floor and a silver candelabrum beside the bed which bore his crest.

The windows were open to the night, and the stars and moon that shone above Delphi threw their silver rays over them.

It was then, very gently, that Lord Warburton undid the evening-gown which Corena had chosen.

Because it was draped very simply in the front, it might have been made for Aphrodite herself.

Then, as she stood looking up at him, her eyes filled with moonlight and her love, he pulled out the pins that held her hair, so that it fell over her shoulders.

Her gown slowly slipped to the floor, and he stood back to look at her.

She was not shy because for the moment she was not herself but the goddess he believed her to be.

She knew, too, that he was not only loving her but worshipping her.

"How can anyone be more beautiful?" he murmured, and his voice was hoarse.

He did not move, but went on:

"I am afraid to touch you in case you are, after all, but a dream, and not real."

It was then Corena found her voice.

"I am . . . very real, my darling husband . . . and I love . . . you!"

As if she could wait no longer, she moved towards him.

Then his arms went round her and his lips found hers.

He kissed her until she felt once again as if the valley, the mountains, all were revolving around them.

They were part of the "Shining Cliffs" and the Temple of Apollo, and there was nothing else in the world but them and their love.

Lord Warburton lifted her into the bed, and as she lay in the soft silken sheets, she could see the stars of Orion in the sky.

She knew they would guide her and help her in everything she did, and in everything she thought.

Then Lord Warburton was beside her, and she felt his arms go round her, his athletic body laid against the softness of hers.

"I love you, my beautiful, perfect little Aphrodite."

"And I . . . love you, Orion . . . although to me you will . . . always be . . . Apollo bringing me light . . . safety and . . . love."

"I worship you and want you, but I am afraid of frightening you."

"How could I ever be . . . frightened of Apollo?" Corena whispered. "I am yours already . . . but . . . darling, I want to be not only . . . a goddess, but your . . . wife."

She realised that her words excited Lord Warburton, and his kisses were no longer gentle and tender, but fierce, demanding, passionate.

Corena was not afraid; she knew they were already one in mind, heart, and soul.

He kissed her eyes, her neck, and then her breasts until she stirred beneath him.

Then, as he made her his, there was a dancing shimmering flame of light, glittering and shining in the air around them.

With it was a mysterious quivering, the beating of silver wings, and the whirling of silver wheels.

They were one with the gods, and there was nothing in the whole world but love.

Barbara Cartland, the world's most famous romantic novelist, who is also an historian, playwright, lecturer, political speaker and television personality, has now written over 460 books and sold over 500 million books the world over.

She has also had many historical works published and has written four autobiographies as well as the biographies of her mother and that of her brother, Ronald Cartland, who was the first Member of Parliament to be killed in the last war. This book has a preface by Sir Winston Churchill and has just been republished with an introduction by Sir Arthur Bryant.

Love at the Helm, a novel written with the help

and inspiration of the late Admiral of the Fleet, the Earl Mountbatten of Burma, is being sold for the Mountbatten Memorial Trust.

Miss Cartland in 1978 sang an Album of Love Songs with the Royal Philharmonic Orchestra.

In 1976 by writing twenty-one books, she broke the world record and has continued for the following nine years with twenty-four, twenty, twenty-three, twenty-four, twenty-four, twenty-five, twenty-three, twenty-six, and twenty-two. She is in the *Guinness Book of Records* as the best-selling author in the world.

She is unique in that she was one and two in the Dalton List of Best Sellers, and one week had four books in the top twenty.

In private life Barbara Cartland, who is a Dame of the Order of St. John of Jerusalem, Chairman of the St. John Council in Hertfordshire and Deputy President of the St. John Ambulance Brigade, has also fought for better conditions and salaries for Midwives and Nurses.

Barbara Cartland is deeply interested in Vitamin Therapy and is President of the British National Association for Health. Her book *The Magic of Honey* has sold throughout the world and is translated into many languages. Her designs "Decorating with Love" are being sold all over the U.S., and the National Home Fashions League named her in 1981, "Woman of Achievement."

In 1984 she received at Kennedy Airport America's Bishop Wright Air Industry Award for her contribution to the development of aviation; in 1931 she and two R.A.F. Officers thought of, and carried, the first aeroplane-towed glider air-mail.

Barbara Cartland's Romances (a book of cartoons) has been published in Great Britain and the U.S.A., as well as a cookery book, *The Romance of Food*, and *Getting Older, Growing Younger*. She has recently written a children's pop-up picture book, entitled *Princess to the Rescue*.

In January 1988 she received "La Médaille de Vermeil de la Ville de Paris." This is the highest award to be given in France by the City of Paris.